The Male Lead is Mine

VOLUME I

KKAMANG KKAMANG

𝒸𝒸 | WORDEXCERPT

Copyright

The Male Lead Is Mine
Kkamang Kkamang
Translation by Dhira Tjoe
Edited by MSM

Visit us at:
wordexcerpt.com
facebook.com/wordexcerpt
twitter.com/wordexcerpt
instagram.com/wordexcerpt

First Edition: November 2021

She had only written to him a handful of times, but each letter had made a lasting impression on his heart. He considered them far too precious to be dismissed in the manner he'd dealt with letters he'd received from other ladies in the past. Why was that? What made this lady so special to him?

PROLOGUE

After finishing the book, the girl had naught but one thing to say: she missed out on a good thing.

The main character of the novel she had just read was the illegitimate daughter of a marquis and worked as a maid in her father's home.

One day, a royal decree was sent to the marquis, stating that he must marry off his daughter to a soldier. Despite being of common birth, the soldier had accomplished many feats in battle and was waiting to be bestowed a formal title.

The emperor sought to bring this talented and renowned soldier into his political faction, and so he searched for a suitable noble household for him to marry into. Eventually, he decided on the family of the marquis, who'd long been one of his loyal supporters.

However, the daughter of the marquis refused to marry a commoner and fled from home. With no other options left and the royal decree sitting heavy on his shoulders, the marquis accepted his illegitimate daughter—the maid—as his child, and married her off to the soldier.

The soldier owned a silo with grain so plentiful he would never have to worry about money a day in his life. Not only that, he was also rumored throughout the nation to be an exceedingly handsome man. Thanks to his wartime achievements, he received a pension from the royal government as well. He had a good personality and was in excellent health.

Of course, the soldier later came to know the truth about his bride, but he did not care about her past. He treated her so well that no one would ever suspect that she had once been a mere maid. Together, they began a loving relationship and lived happily ever after.

The runaway daughter, on the other hand, had met a terrible man in the streets and suffered severe physical and emotional distress. One day, she happened to meet the man who she had been meant to marry and fell in love with his good looks. Although she attempted to win the soldier over by insisting that she was his true bride, he saw through her act and threw her out of his estate.

Most people would favor the main character of a book, but the girl sympathized with the runaway daughter instead. She felt sorry for her.

See, you shouldn't have rejected him.

With that final thought, the girl shut the book gently and fell asleep.

The Male Lead Is Mine

When the girl awoke, she found herself in unfamiliar surroundings. Wrapped around her was a soft, fluffy blanket, and, from her bed, she could see an ornate coat of arms.

She had never seen any of this before.

"What on earth..?"

It was undeniably bizarre. Suddenly, memories and thoughts not her own began filling her mind—she was becoming one with someone else.

"Aaaah!!!" she screamed.

Everything hurt; her head felt like it would split in half. Startled by the girl's screams, maids came rushing in from the hall.

"My lady!"

"Are you all right?"

The girl clutched her head and looked at the maids and their black, Western-style dresses with white frills. As she recognized these dresses as maid uniforms, she laughed in disbelief.

"Excuse me..."

"Yes, my lady?"

"I'm the only daughter of Marquis Ian Horissen, right?"

The maids glanced at each other in confusion before nodding. "That is correct."

"My God!" she exclaimed.

She had become the misfortunate Lady Aris Horissen, the character she pitied the most.

She got out of bed and examined her small, pretty hands, then ran toward the nearest mirror. There, in her reflection, stood a girl who couldn't have been more than ten.

"I'm younger now," she muttered.

Not only had she gotten younger, but she'd become prettier as well. This was to be expected, as Aris Horissen would later try to charm and seduce the male lead with her beauty.

The girl clenched her fist tightly.

She wouldn't let her fate be decided by the plot of a novel.

She would live a new life.

CROWN PRINCESS

"What are the accomplishments of Emperor Goji?"

"In order to stabilize the lives of the people, he ordered the nobles to purchase manure in large quantities. This allowed citizens to obtain fertilizer at a lower cost and thus they were able to prolong the harvest season."

"That is correct."

The professor looked at his student, pleased. He was proud of her for remembering what he'd taught her yesterday and found her to be an exceptional student. For a girl of only sixteen, she was quite mature and behaved admirably during class.

She studied continuously in order to retain all of the day's learning. While she was not a genius or a prodigy, she worked hard enough to make up for any shortcomings. The professor preferred this type of quiet, obedient student over those who were clever but arrogant.

"Today, we will be learning about Emperor Goji's other accomplishments," he began.

"Yes, professor."

There was much more to learn about Emperor Goji. The girl prepared to take notes as the professor lectured her about his history on the chalkboard.

Tying her brown hair into a neat ponytail, her chocolate eyes raptly followed the professor's every movement. She was completely and utterly focused on the task at hand.

"Class is over for today. Your homework is just to copy your notes on the content from today's lecture."

The girl was planning on doing so whether the professor had assigned it to her or not. She found it difficult to remember times in history if she didn't remember what came from the past.

"Thank you, professor,"

"The pleasure is mine."

As the professor left with a small bow, the girl sighed and dropped the gracious smile from her face.

She sighed. "How boring."

The professor was wise but painfully dull. She barely managed to stay awake during his lectures.

"When am I ever going to finish all of this?" she grumbled. She couldn't help but grumble; the amount of work he gave her every lesson was enormous, not to mention how draining it was to keep up with it all class after class.

The amount of work required for the professor's lessons was enormous, and it took an even greater amount of effort for the girl to keep up with it all. She was not fond of history, but she was required to learn it as a member of the aristocracy.

The Male Lead Is Mine

"Lady Aris!" a maid said, stepping into the room.

Her name was Lucine, and she was the main character of the original novel.

"What's next?"

"Your dance lessons, my lady."

The day's events were identical to those of yesterday, and they'd be the same tomorrow as well as on the day after that. She would wake up, go to history lessons in the morning, eat lunch, then go to dancing lessons in the afternoon. After that, she would eat dinner, finish her homework, then go to sleep.

She had thought being a lady meant she'd be able to sleep, eat, and play all day, but that couldn't have been further from reality. There was so much to do and so many lectures to attend. Thankfully, she wasn't being tested on the material, but she still disliked studying—she simply felt there was no need for it.

In the original novel, Aris Horissen hated schoolwork. She refused to study and forced Lucine to do her homework in her stead. Thanks to that, Lucine became a well-educated and cultured woman despite her birth status. That wouldn't happen this time.

When the girl first woke up in the novel, she was given all of Aris Horissen's memories and knowledge of the world. This allowed her to create a new, better version of Aris.

With the old Aris' knowledge of this world, it wasn't hard for her to adjust to her new life in the novel. However, just because she became Aris Horissen didn't mean she would live the life scripted for her.

Everything I do is to change the outcome of the story.

She smiled and took a sip of the tea Lucine had brought for her; the interesting flavor pleased her.

"This is nice."

"Isn't it?"

"Mhm."

Aris looked at Lucine. She was a bright, spunky girl. Though illegitimate, she could have been accepted into the family if the head of the household allowed it, but the marquis refused.

She had a pretty—if rather plain—face and a certain charming aura. Her blue hair and yellow eyes shone brightly. No wonder the male lead grew to like her, even after finding out she was of lowly birth.

Even I like Lucine, she mused.

After her classes, Aris would be completely worn out. Lucine, who had a keen eye for these things, often brought her tea and snacks to cheer her up.

"I feel my fatigue disappearing thanks to your tea, Lucine."

"Were you exhausted?"

She smiled, intentionally omitting her thoughts about how boring it had been. "Well, it's not easy to be in class for three hours."

Lucine wasn't the type of girl who spread rumors, but it was still best not to say anything that could be twisted later on—just in case.

Aris took another sip of her tea and Lucine asked, "Do you have a lot of homework today?"

"Yes. Do you want to learn with me?"

Lucine shook her head at Aris' words. "I'm just a maid, miss."

In the kingdom they lived in, education was not a right, but a privilege. The upper class could afford tutors and professors, but common people had no way of learning, especially as mandatory schooling had yet to be established. Education was a symbol of privilege—without money, one could not gain access to it. Studying was something only wealthy heirs or nobles could do.

The novel's male lead, however, had been lucky. Despite his family's financial difficulties, his parents sent him to an academy where he excelled in swordsmanship. His skills greatly surpassed those of any other commoner, and he became somewhat of a legend at the academy.

After completing his schooling, he became the hero of the battlefield and accomplished amazing feats for the good of the kingdom. Although the emperor had offered to bestow him a title, he refused and retreated to his estate in the countryside, saying he did not care for politics.

The male lead had a favorable reputation and was exceptionally skilled. The emperor, who knew this well, wanted to ensure his bloodline's loyalty to the throne and decided to marry him into one of his supporters' families. The girl who was chosen to be his bride was none other than Lady Horissen.

Me. I'm the one who was chosen.

Since rumors were inevitable, Aris decided she'd rather have good rumors than bad ones and did the complete opposite of what the original Lady Horissen had done. She had once looked into her rumors and was pleased to find out that her only reputation was that of a beautiful and sophisticated young lady.

Aris, who had been eating cookies absentmindedly, reached for another, only to find the plate was empty. She wanted more, and that did not escape her maid's eyes.

"You still need to eat lunch later, my lady. You shouldn't have too many cookies," Lucine said gently as if reading the girl's mind.

"Okay."

Aris ate very little in order to maintain her figure. She didn't gain weight easily but found that she tended to fatten up if she didn't watch herself. She had learned this lesson the hard way and vowed to never let it happen again.

As Aris descended to the lower floor for lunch, she spotted her father, Ian, already seated at the dining table.

"Father!" she exclaimed, beaming brightly.

In the original novel, Aris and her father had not been close. The marquis was constantly disappointed with his thoughtless daughter and tried to change her, but Aris felt that he nagged too much and grew to dislike him.

"Aris, you're here."

Things were different now. After the girl had become Aris Horissen, she had taken painstaking measures to ensure she had a spotless reputation. Ian knew this as well. He was a rather stony, taciturn man, but he would melt in front of his daughter. How could he remain silent when his daughter was as lovely and adorable as she was?

"Did you have a good lunch, Father?"

"It was all right."

"You need to make sure you're eating well!" Aris said to her father, smiling.

She liked Ian well enough and thought he was a good man. At the very least, he was a father who loved her just for trying her best.

"I will."

Ian's face brightened at Aris' affectionate chiding, and he smiled gently. Aris lowered her head. The first time she had done this, he hadn't known how to react, but now he knew exactly what she wanted. He brought a hand up and patted her head, smoothing her silky brown hair with his fingers.

"Are you going to the palace today?"

"I am."

She had yet to go to the palace, but she had heard countless rumors about it. The rumor she liked the most was that there was a garden with flowers constantly in bloom.

Aris had always longed to go to the palace, but she had yet to be formally invited. Every time her Father went there, she thought of the garden filled with ever-blooming flowers.

Ian looked up at her with a warm smile and said, "Come home safely."

"I will." Aris grinned at him and turned her attention to the plate of tender meat and roasted vegetables the chef had brought out for her.

Ian watched her eat for a moment, then got up from the table, saying, "Well, I'll leave you to finish your meal."

"Yes, Father."

She gave him one last smile, noting with delight how her normally stoic father seemed to brighten at her expression. Thanks to her constant displays of affection, Ian was practically wrapped around her little finger.

"I'm sure he'll bring home an excellent suitor for me one day," she murmured to herself.

If all went according to the original plot, the marquis would come home bearing the news of her engagement to the male lead. However, Aris knew things could change. She had, after all, changed her entire life to benefit her.

From the moment she transmigrated, she'd cultivated an image as an earnest, hardworking girl and not some silly good-for-nothing. This allowed her to earn respect and admiration from her father and those around her.

The only way to find a worthy suitor was to have good social standing. Looks meant next to nothing in the grand scheme of things. While Aris was a beautiful girl, she wasn't the beauty of the century by any means.

Any man worth marrying would consider his future wife's reputation. After all, she would be the woman he'd spend the rest of his life with. It was only natural that he would look for someone with a decent upbringing and looks, but, most importantly, a good personality.

Every action Aris took was for her future and to ultimately gain the affection of the male lead. She wondered just how handsome he was for the Aris Horissen to have fallen for him at first sight.

I'm so curious.

However, there were still two-and-a-half years left before she would start receiving any offers of marriage. The original Aris Horissen had received her first offer when she turned nineteen years old. She would have to find a way to make the next two-and-a-half years go by faster.

I'd like to go to the palace too, she thought.

After she became a lady and got exposed daily to plenty of finery and elegance, Aris grew interested in such things. She wanted to sit within the palace gardens and enjoy high tea while admiring the blossoms someday.

Actually, I changed my mind.

In this world, coffee was a rarity—a precious delicacy afforded only to the upper class. Even the marquis only had it once or twice a month.

Coffee. I'm going to have coffee in the garden, not tea.

She liked this adjustment. After finishing the rest of her meal, she got up from her seat, prompting maids to file in to clear the table.

"Thanks," she said before leaving.

This was the best way to get the maids to like her.

"Of course, miss."

Aris was pleased with their response.

Her next lessons were for dance. When a lady of the nobility turned seventeen, it was customary for her to enter high society by throwing a debutante ball at the palace. As Aris was already sixteen, she needed to learn how to dance. Thankfully, she was naturally graceful and could follow the steps with ease.

Once she arrived at the third floor, Aris bowed to her dance instructor. It was a woman in her late thirties, and she was the most highly regarded dance instructor in the capital. Ian had specially invited her to teach Aris—he wanted only the best teachers for his little girl.

He never expressed it, but Ian loved his daughter terribly. The only person who didn't know this was the original Aris. Ian had only accepted the marriage between Aris and the male lead after making sure he was a man worthy of his daughter in the first place.

The original Aris would never know that.

"Good afternoon," she said with a cordial smile.

She had practiced this smile countless times in the mirror; it was the smile that made her look the most beautiful.

"You're always smiling whenever I see you, Lady Horissen," the instructor said, happy to see her. She was quite fond of her pupil, as the young lady always made such an effort to remember everything she'd learned the day before. "Did you practice late into the night again?"

"Of course."

Aris always made her efforts known. She would never practice her dancing in secret; instead, she made sure all the maids knew she was dancing. She had to show everyone around her how hard she was trying.

The dance instructor was fully aware of this as well. As Aris responded eagerly, the instructor's cheeks flushed. How confident and delightful she was!

"The dance we will learn today is not for standard balls, but rather for masquerades, or when you are dancing with someone in private," said the instructor.

"Oh my."

"I must warn you, it's rather risqué."

"I want to learn it!" Aris replied, excited.

"How odd! Most other ladies say they don't want to learn it for that very reason!"

"I think it's good to learn a variety of things."

"You're quite correct."

After delivering the perfect response, Aris smiled innocently. She was looking forward to learning the racy dance. She'd have to commit it all to memory and practice it again later that night.

Today, like every other day, Aris gained the adoration of everyone around her.

The Male Lead Is Mine

Ian gazed at the palace, which stood imposingly in the distance. He was drawing ever closer to it, transported by a carriage sporting the Horissen family crest. He was heading toward the palace's Eastern Gate; the entrance used by nobles and other members of the court.

Today, there would be a meeting to discuss candidates for the title of crown princess. The crown prince would soon be of age and he would need a bride. Ian thought of his daughter, Aris, who had smiled at him so brightly before he'd left.

My daughter is still so young, he lamented.

He knew she would soon become a debutante, but she was too young to get married to the crown prince.

In the Republic of Xenon, most men married in their late twenties, while most women married in their early twenties. Considering this societal norm, Aris was still far too young—but she wasn't just any citizen. Children of nobles typically got betrothed in their teens and married in their early twenties. Ian knew this applied to Aris as well, but his mind could not help but still consider her just a little girl.

As the carriage came to a halt, the coachman opened the door for the marquis. Ian stepped out with his private guard, and the two slowly walked toward the Central Palace where the meeting would be held. Alongside them were other nobles, presumably all heading in the same direction he was.

Upon arriving at the Central Palace, Ian slowly made his way through the halls. The corridor was filled with sunlight, and Ian basked in its warmth as he breathed in the fresh spring air.

"Marquis Horissen."

Ian's reverie was interrupted by a man calling his name. He turned and saw a man with shining blond hair and blue eyes standing before him.

"Duke Essel, Your Excellency."

The man was Louison d'Essel, Duke of Essel. He was close in age to Marquis Horissen and, while they were on a first-name basis privately, they were in court. The two took care to maintain etiquette when they were in formal settings.

"I hear the emperor has an announcement to make about the crown prince," Duke Essel began.

"Yes, I'm aware."

"How are you feeling?"

"About what?"

"Your daughter could be a candidate for crown princess."

Ian choked at Louison's words. "She's too young."

"Isn't she sixteen?"

"Precisely. Aris is too young," Ian insisted. "Perhaps your daughter will become a candidate, Duke Essel."

"What?" the Duke asked incredulously. "My daughter is thirteen."

Louison's daughter, Violet d'Essel, was three years younger than Aris. It was far more likely that Aris would be chosen over Violet, but, with a calm smile, Ian said, "She's only six years younger than the crown prince."

Aris was not much younger than the crown prince either, but Ian stared at Louison unwaveringly. Both men were entirely certain their daughter would never be chosen to become the crown princess.

"My daughter still needs to get older."

"As does my daughter, Your Excellency," Ian replied.

With that, the two men headed to the conference hall together.

Juselle Ren Xenon, the emperor of the Xenon Empire, studied the list he held very closely. It contained the names of the most beautiful and well-bred ladies in the capital. Next to their names, there was a brief profile of each lady. The list of names had almost as many people as there were attendees to today's conference.

"Let's go."

"Yes, Your Imperial Majesty."

As the emperor strode toward the conference hall, his gentlemen-in-waiting followed him with several copies of the list. The nobles had already gathered inside the hall. Marquis Horissen was the first to rise and greet the emperor, and the other nobles followed suit.

Acknowledging their greetings, Juselle sat on his throne and said, "Take a seat."

As soon as everyone was seated, the gentlemen-in-waiting began distributing the list to each attendee. The nobles stared in bewilderment at the papers they were receiving.

"As you're all aware, the crown prince will turn nineteen soon, and there will be a ball in his honor," Juselle said grandly.

"Yes, Your Imperial Majesty."

"The crown prince shall choose one of the ladies on this list to dance with at the ball."

Everyone quickly diverted their attention to the document before them. Some faces brightened at the prospect of their daughters having the opportunity to dance with the crown prince. There was a chance he would find one of them pleasing, perhaps even choosing to pursue a future with them.

Some were disappointed to see that their daughters were not on the list, while others had entirely different reactions.

"Your Imperial Majesty, if I may?" Ian spoke up first.

"Speak, Marquis Horissen."

"Why is my daughter on this list?"

"I have heard that she is both beautiful and kind and that she is more than fit to be listed here," the emperor replied.

Most people had one or two faults, but his investigation revealed that everyone had nothing but praise for Lady Aris. That was why Juselle had listed her on the first page. She was rumored to be a fine, upstanding young lady of noble heritage, not to mention she was the daughter of Marquis Horissen, a devoted supporter of the crown.

"Your Imperial Majesty, please remove her from the list," the marquis pleaded, less than happy about seeing his daughter's name.

Emperor Juselle was shocked. He could not believe what he was hearing—Ian wanted to pass up the opportunity of having his daughter become the crown princess?

"My daughter is too young!" Ian exclaimed.

As he began to protest, Juselle gave him a look of disbelief. Next to him, Louison raised his hand. After all, his daughter Violet was on the list as well. Although she was young, she was not young enough to be excluded from consideration.

The Male Lead Is Mine

"My daughter is only thirteen!" Louison exclaimed. "Duke Essel."

"Please remove her from the list."

The two men wanted to ensure that their daughters would not be chosen. As soon as they began to protest, so did other members of the nobility. Apparently, they all deeply cared for their daughters.

Although they knew the title of crown princess was a great honor, many nobles began backing out, saying that their daughters, too, were still too young.

Juselle looked at his quickly decreasing list and made a decision. "I will not allow anyone to be removed from the list solely because of their age."

Juselle had secretly hoped that either the daughter of Marquis Horissen or Duke Essel would be chosen. They both came from noble bloodlines and were loyal to the current royal family. They did not have much political ambition, and Juselle was sure they would help strengthen the crown.

He had many expectations from the two men, but now they were begging him to remove their daughters from the list. It had nothing to do with their loyalty to him and everything to do with their love for their daughters.

At that moment, the door flung open, and a young man came in. His blond hair, similar in color to Juselle's, grazed just past his shoulders as his blue eyes shone like the sky. He was extremely handsome, the spitting image of the emperor. It was the crown prince, Hiel Ren Xenon.

The crown prince looked around. "What's going on here?"

Juselle and all of the nobles in attendance watched as the crown prince picked up the list of eligible ladies and began flipping through the pages.

"I heard I'm supposed to select my partner for my first dance at the ball," the crown prince said.

"That is correct."

"That's why I'm here."

Juselle looked at Hiel. To his knowledge, his son was not in a relationship, nor did he nurture special affections for any girl in particular. From an early age, Hiel learned that his future wife would be chosen for him. He had never felt the need to start a romantic relationship or approach the opposite sex. Thus, the current list of eligible ladies came to be.

"Is there a problem?" Hiel asked, scanning the list. "They all seem to be very charming young ladies."

"Of course. I compiled the list myself," the emperor boasted.

"Then I'm happy with it."

What Hiel was actually happy about was the abundance of women for him to choose from. He had no idea there were so many beautiful, smart, and good-natured women living in the capital. Recently, he had grown bored of how his mistresses quarreled over him, so this was the perfect opportunity to find a new plaything.

"It would be such a shame to reject all of the fine young ladies you chose," Hiel mused for a moment. He then perked up, as if he had an idea. "What if I invited them to a tea party? Then I could meet them all and then choose the lady I'll dance with at the ball. How does that sound?"

Ian and Louison went pale. Their daughters, meeting the crown prince? They were still too young to meet any men, let alone a potential husband. But the two friends were not the only ones who looked uneasy. Everyone who had protested against their daughters being on the list began to look a little sick.

"Hmm…" Juselle pondered for a moment, then nodded his head in agreement. "You are the one who will be dancing with the young lady, so I suppose she must fit your standards."

The emperor felt Hiel had made a good suggestion. "Marquis Horissen," he called.

"Yes, Your Majesty."

"Duke Essel!"

"Yes, Your Majesty."

"This is a royal decree. Your daughters, and everyone else's daughters, must be in attendance at the tea party!" Juselle ordered.

If even one person could remove their daughter from the list, everyone would want to do the same. Before this, the emperor had no idea that the nobles treasured their daughters so much.

Ian and Louison exchanged a glance. Both were desperately thinking of ways to ensure their children would not be summoned to the palace, but neither man could come up with a plan. They could not argue against the emperor, and that knowledge shrouded their features with the shadow of defeat.

All they could do was inform their daughters about the royal decree.

A man led his horse at a brisk pace, long black hair gently waving in the breeze. His blue eyes, shining like the stars in the sky, surveyed his surroundings: a battle-field littered with the bodies of enemy soldiers. Brushing his hair away from his eyes, he slowly turned his horse around.

"Commander Roy," a voice called out to him. It came from one of the surviving members of his troops.

The soldier walked toward him, clicking his tongue as he saw the carnage around them. It was as though his commander's sword was a harbinger of death.

"You're unbelievable," the soldier said in awe.

Roy smiled bitterly, but it only seemed to enhance his already handsome features.

"Everything happened exactly as you said it would, sir."

This operation—Roy's operation—had been a re-sounding success. Victories while under his command happened so often that hardly anyone was surprised at this point.

"There's a new letter waiting for you, sir," the soldier continued.

It was common for Roy to receive letters. Although he did receive the occasional message from his friends, most of his correspondences came from common folk or young women enamored with his heroism.

"Right," he said, treading ahead. "They all expect responses, don't they?"

"Ah…"

"These letters are becoming a pain," Roy said, shaking his head slowly. He didn't know what to make of his sudden and bewildering popularity, so he simply burned most of the letters he received after reading them. These kinds of letters came often and always requested that he reply to them. However, he lacked the time and desire to write back to a complete stranger.

"Let's go back," he sighed wearily, and the soldier nodded. Roy led his horse forward slowly.

The day's battle was over.

Aris stifled another yawn and paid closer attention to the class... or at least pretended to. History class was as tedious as always, and pretending to be attentive was an act she was used to putting up. Whenever she felt herself slipping into slumber, she would pinch the back of her hand as hard as she could, trying to stay awake. She was just glad the professor allowed her to have a small break mid-class.

With how big of a breakfast she'd eaten this morning, it was undoubtedly the cause of her sleepiness. As time went on, it was becoming increasingly challenging for her to keep her eyes open. The moment the professor stepped out of the room for a break, Aris took the opportunity to stand up and stretch vigorously. She could only do this when she was by herself, never while in sight of the professor.

Lucine entered with tea and snacks. The tea she brewed was always delicious, and Aris always looked forward to having it.

"Have some tea, my lady." The maid offered.

"Alright."

The tea was sweet, with a delicate fragrance. Aris took a sip and then bit into a soft cookie.

"The Marquis asks that you join him in his study after your lessons."

"The study?" Aris frowned.

Her father rarely called her to his study, and she couldn't help but wonder if something had happened.

Aris tilted her head.

According to the novel, nothing major was supposed to happen to her at this point in her life. Of course, the story started when she turned nineteen. Still, if anything significant had occurred in her past, it would have surely been mentioned.

I don't know what it could possibly be.

After she had transmigrated into the novel, Aris' destiny had changed drastically. She was held in high regard by everyone, with a reputation of being an honest, hardworking girl. Perhaps she had changed so much that other elements of the story had changed as well.

I haven't even made my debut yet.

There was no way that she'd be receiving a marriage proposal. Not at her age, she thought as she sipped her tea. Once the break ended, the professor returned, smelling heavily of smoke and tobacco. It seemed he'd gone out for a cigar.

Ugh, gross.

She wanted to tell him to quit smoking, but she knew it was easier said than done.

At least he had the decency to go smoke outside, she thought, and smiled despite her mild displeasure.

"Do you remember where we left off?" he asked.

"Yes, Professor."

"You seem a little tired today," the professor noted.

"It's very embarrassing, but I believe I'm somewhat drowsy today because I overate during breakfast. My apologies, sir. This won't happen again," she murmured while daintily covering her mouth with one hand.

The professor nodded and patted her shoulder, saying, "It's no problem at all, I understand."

He left the matter at that and carried on with his lesson. Aris focused on her studies while taking small sips of tea. She was glad Lucine had left it there for her; with it, she did not fall asleep again.

By the time Aris was done with her lessons, it was already evening. She figured it would be best to speak to Ian before dinner and headed toward the study, with Lucine following close behind. Two knights were guarding the door, but when Aris approached, they granted her entry.

"Father, it's me, Aris," she announced before entering.

Ian, who had been organizing papers at his desk, stood to greet his daughter. "Come, have a seat," he said, gesturing toward one of the sofas in the study. Once Aris was settled, he sat down across from her.

"I'll bring some tea," Lucine said before scurrying out. Aris studied Ian's expression—it didn't look like he had good news for her.

"What's wrong?" Aris asked. Ian seemed to be struggling to form a response.

"Your tea," Lucine said, setting down a tea set and a platter of treats. "I'll leave you both to speak now."

She left, shutting the door quietly behind her.

Ian let out a small sigh and took a sip of the tea before saying, "There will be a celebration ball for the crown prince soon."

"Yes, I heard."

She had also heard that a candidate for crown princess would be selected on that day but paid little attention. It wasn't something that involved her.

"The emperor made a list of candidates for the next crown princess, and... your name was on that list."

"Excuse me?" Aris blinked, not having expected him to say that of all things. She set her tea down and pointed at herself incredulously, "You mean... me?"

"That's right."

She was astonished. "My God."

She had cleaned up her act and tried to build a favorable reputation, only for it to land her on a list of crown princess candidates. The crown princess wasn't even a character in the original novel—she'd never been mentioned. The author had only written about the love story between the male lead and Lucine. So, then, why was she being considered for Crown Princess?

"There were many girls on the list besides you, too," Ian added.

"The emperor made this list himself?"

"He did."

Aris had been placed in a carefully curated register of the most eligible ladies in the capital, and, somehow, this made her very pleased. While she had no desire to become the next crown princess, it still pleased her for some reason to know that people knew she could. However...

"What's the issue?"

"It's not that. The real issue is just..." Ian trailed off.

"Yes?"

Ian held her hand tightly, hesitating.

"Just tell me, Father."

The Male Lead Is Mine

"...The crown prince was supposed to choose a dance partner for the upcoming ball from that list. But, instead, he decided to invite every single lady on that list to a tea party."

"Ah."

"I tried saying you were too young, but it was no use."

That must be the reason her father looked so distraught—his little girl had been selected as a candidate for crown princess.

Aris nodded in understanding. "What kind of person is the crown prince?" she asked.

Having never paid much attention to the palace's workings, she knew next to nothing about the prince.

"He's a very calculating man."

"Calculating?" she repeated.

"He's quite fond of women, but only takes them as mistresses."

Suddenly, Aris' mouth was filled with an acrid taste. The crown prince sounded like the type of man she did not want to associate with. She took another sip of tea and smiled thinly.

"Since we are a noble household, and you are such a beautiful and sweet girl, the emperor seemingly wanted you to become the crown princess," Ian added.

"Oh my." She hadn't expected that.

"Either you or Louison's daughter."

"Ah, the young lady?"

"Yes." Her father nodded.

She had heard rumors of how the girl had just celebrated her thirteenth birthday and of her astonishing beauty.

The original novel had not mentioned who the crown princess was. After all, the main characters of the novel were the male lead and Lucine.

"When is the tea party?" Aris asked.

"Next week."

"Oh, there's not much time left then."

Aris mulled over her thoughts for a moment, noting that she would need to get fitted for a new dress. She would also need to decide what kind of makeup she would wear.

Ian's expression seemed to darken. "If only I had more power… then you wouldn't have to go through this."

"Well. This will be quite a headache for me," she admitted.

Realizing that he would be sending his daughter to a place she didn't want to go, Ian paled.

"Where will the tea party be held?"

"Since it is a special occasion, it will be held in the Spring Garden, where flowers bloom constantly," he explained.

"The Spring Garden?"

"That's right."

The Spring Garden was one of the most stunning gardens in the palace. Flowers bloomed there year-round, giving the illusion of eternal spring. Aris had always wanted to see it in person, having seen only illustrations of it in newspapers.

This could be a good experience for her. She was growing tired of being cooped up at home anyway. If she was to be forced to attend the crown prince's tea party, she might as well take a detour and check out the Spring Garden.

The Male Lead Is Mine

There's no way I'd be selected anyway, she thought, lifting her teacup to her lips. *Ooh, perfect form*—

It was only yesterday that she had learned tea etiquette, and she'd spent the entire night practicing the proper motions. All that practice seemed to have paid off; her table manners were executed with the utmost poise and grace.

"Don't worry, Father. I'm sure there will be ladies far prettier than I am, and the crown prince may not even find me to his liking," she said to Ian reassuringly.

Her sweet words somewhat calmed him.

"I suppose that is a possibility…"

"Anyway, I heard that Lady Violet was quite the beauty. I'm sure the crown prince will be drawn to the most gorgeous lady in attendance."

"But how can any woman be more beautiful than my daughter?"

Aris smiled bashfully at his words. Sure, in her father's eyes, she might seem like the most beautiful girl in the world, but she saw herself objectively.

She had appealing features, but that was about it. She wasn't a breathtaking beauty with flowing golden hair and twinkling sapphire eyes. She was just another girl with plain brown hair and dull brown eyes.

Within the Xenon Empire, the standard of beauty was to have blond hair and blue eyes. Aris, born with brown hair and equally brown eyes, did not quite fit that standard. She had heard that Violet had shimmering blond hair and eyes as blue as the ocean, and figured the crown prince would prefer her over Aris.

She relayed her thoughts to her father. "I know I'm not ugly, but Lady Violet is blond and has blue eyes."

"That's right."

"And what about the crown prince's mistresses? Are many of them blonde?" she asked.

"The majority are," he agreed, nodding.

"Then we have nothing to worry about!"

At Aris' cheerful words, Ian smiled.

She had a point.

"You're right."

He silently apologized to Louison and proceeded to enjoy high tea with his daughter.

"You were invited to the palace?" Lucine squealed with excitement. She couldn't believe it; Lady Aris had not even debuted yet, but she was already receiving invitations! "But your dress! What will you wear?"

Lucine began going over her mental catalog of her lady's wardrobe. They were pretty enough to be worn every day, but they were far too simple for visiting the palace. Most palace women wore exquisite dresses with low, swooping necklines.

"You should get fitted for a new dress first thing in the morning, my lady!" Lucine said, concerned.

"I was thinking that too."

"Then you really should get some rest," Lucine said, watching Aris study late as always. "I think you should postpone all of your classes for now. You'll need at least a week to prepare for the palace."

There was much to prepare before the palace visit. Not only did Aris need to be dressed to the nines, but so did Lucine. No matter how extravagantly a lady dressed up, she would surely attract criticism if her maid looked shabby and unkempt.

"Get some rest!" Lucine nagged.

"Well… all right," Aris said, shutting her books with a tiny smile. Since she had decided to postpone classes for a week, she didn't have to complete her homework for tomorrow. "I really should finish this though…"

"It will be fine! You're always so diligent, I'm sure nothing will happen just because you didn't do your homework for a day."

"Right?" Aris replied, relieved.

The idea of not attending history classes for an entire week excited her. She tried not to let it show on the outside and pretended to sigh heavily before climbing into her bed.

"Should I turn the lights off, my lady?"

"Yes."

Lucine turned off the lamp and exited the bedchambers.

Finally alone, Aris stared at the ceiling and murmured to herself, "What's going to happen to me now?"

She had tried so hard to change her fate, but now things weren't going as expected. Who would have imagined that she would be selected as a candidate to be the crown princess?

"I need to be careful," she murmured.

The mere thought of becoming the crown prince's wife gave her a full-body shudder. The prince was not a loyal man, what with him having several mistresses around. He would probably treat her with as much respect as her position deserved, but that was not what Aris wanted.

Not to mention that if she married the prince, she would become the empress someday. The position entailed so many tiresome duties and was such a burdensome role; Aris knew she would never be happy as the empress. She wanted a peaceful and leisurely life.

"Besides, I like the male lead," she chuckled.

He was loyal to the one woman he loved, listened to what she had to say, and always believed in her. What a man!

Unfortunately for Aris, there were still two-and-a-half years left before she could meet him. She had to make it through those years safely. She decided she would keep a low profile at the tea party, take a walk through the Spring Garden, and leave.

There was just one kink in her plan. If the emperor wanted her to become the crown princess, then the crown prince would certainly approach her. What would she do then?

After racking her brains for a suitable answer, she closed her eyes. It was late, and she was getting tired.

I'll figure it out tomorrow.

Aris fell into a deep, peaceful slumber.

The week flew by without Aris even noticing it. She had been too preoccupied with fabrics, jewels, and shoes.

After much deliberation and several trips to the capital's finest dressmakers, Aris had finally decided on a lovely white dress with a ribbon adorning it. The swooping neckline exposed her collarbones and showed just enough skin to be appropriate, while still adhering to the latest trends.

Sixteen might be too young for this dress, she mused.

The dress was better suited for a young woman than a teenager, but Lucine had boldly insisted on it.

"I'm hungry," Aris whined.

"You can't eat yet," Lucine said sternly.

"Can't I have some water, at least?"

"No, my lady!"

Lucine was unrelenting, entirely committed to making sure her lady would be the most beautiful girl in attendance. She even took it upon herself to regulate her eating habits. Aris was restricted to one meal a day to maintain her slender figure, and Lucine would not budge on this rule. Aris had to forfeit her breakfast and lunch to have high tea and dinner.

Why do I have to do all of this?

Aris wanted to cry. She couldn't believe she had to give up her meals to look good for some crown prince. How horrible this situation was!

It was all the crown prince's fault. If he hadn't decided to host his stupid tea party out of the blue, none of this would be happening. And why on earth did he choose to host the party in the evening? It would have been so much better to start the party in the morning and have it done before lunch.

The late start time was because the crown prince had an appointment in the afternoon. This was the best he could do to accommodate everyone's schedules.

"You're not the only person that's hungry, miss."

"Lucine…"

"I'm sure all of the other ladies are as hungry as you right now," Lucine said, offering what support she could. "I haven't even eaten in front of you once!"

"But that doesn't mean you're not eating."

"I can eat because I'm not a lady," Lucine explained as she helped Aris into her dress.

Her brown hair was pinned up, exposing Aris' slender neck and shoulders. The jewels in the bodice twinkled like stars, and the skirt flowed beautifully. Aris always insisted she wasn't that pretty, but, to Lucine, her lady was the most beautiful woman in the world.

"All we need now is to do your makeup," Lucine said.

"Right." Aris nodded weakly.

Having skipped breakfast, she hardly had the energy to stand, let alone speak. She wondered if she would die of hunger on the way to the palace and stared at Lucine balefully.

For a brief moment, Lucine's resolve faltered, but she remembered her ultimate goal. She had to be stern for the sake of her lady.

"Let's start your makeup now," she said firmly.

Aris pouted, realizing her sorrowful expression had made no difference.

A makeup artist entered the room.

"I'm just going to make you a little paler," the woman explained, patting a fragrant powder onto her skin.

Aris glanced at the mirror and saw that she really did look whiter. After applying the powder, the artist tinted her lips with a light coral color. Then, an assortment of pale oranges and warm browns was brushed on her skin. The whole process took far longer than Aris had expected.

"All done," the woman said finally.

When Aris took a good look at herself in the mirror, she was shocked. The girl she saw a few moments ago was gone. Now she looked youthful and sophisticated.

"Since you're still young, I tried not to make you look too sultry," the woman added.

"Oh my," Aris murmured, reaching out to touch her reflection. She wondered how beautiful she would look to everyone else.

At that moment, Ian knocked on the door. "Aris, are you finished?"

"Yes, Father."

Aris was unfamiliar with the palace grounds, so Ian would be escorting her to the Spring Garden.

She sprang up from her seat and put on her coat. The nighttime air was still cold, and she didn't want to risk catching a chill on the way to the palace. When the door opened, Ian, who stood in the doorway, stared at his daughter in surprise.

"My daughter, you look so beautiful."

"Really?"

He nodded. "Yes."

She may not be blond like most beauties, but she was gorgeous regardless. Aris' grin rather stunned her father.

"I'm sure the other ladies will look lovely too."

"Really?"

"The crown prince won't even bother to look at me."

At least, she hoped so.

She linked her arm with her father's and descended the staircase. On the way down, Ian cleared his throat and observed his daughter's appearance. Seeing her dressed like this, he realized that she did not look as young as he thought she was.

But, in any case, he thought, *she's still too young to get married —*

The two stepped into the carriage and set off for the Spring Garden.

A large arrangement of flowers greeted the Horissen's at the entryway. The Spring Garden was just as the rumors had said—there were countless leafy green trees and flowers in bloom as far as the eye could see; it was a floral jubilee. Freesia flower petals, which symbolized spring, drifted dreamily through the breeze. The sight before Aris was so beautiful she felt that perhaps her hunger and pain had been worth it.

"You can go now, Father," she told him since Ian looked worried. "I have Lucine. Everything will be fine."

Around them, other girls began to arrive with their fathers. They also looked a little gloomy, as if they'd been hungry for a long time. All of the girls gazed longingly at the decadent food piled atop the tables. Unfortunately, they could not allow themselves to start eating before the crown prince arrived.

"Be safe," Ian muttered to his daughter.

"I will."

Ian finally left the garden. He was still worried, but he trusted Lucine. As tonight was a special event, and with so many noble ladies present, palace guards were stationed around to ensure maximum security. As soon as Aris saw her father get into the carriage, she made a beeline for the food, but Lucine grabbed her wrist.

"Miss."

"What?"

"You can't eat yet."

"Why not?" Aris whined.

"You haven't shown the crown prince how lovely you look," Lucine said sharply.

She wanted the crown prince to see Aris as she was right now.

"But I'm so hungry," Aris replied weakly.

"You're normally so composed. Just wait a little longer."

"I can't stand being hungry."

Aris could tolerate most things through sheer willpower, but hunger was not one of those things. She gave Lucine her best puppy eyes. "Just a little bit?"

Lucine felt her resolve crumble slightly. "One drink," she relented.

"I'll take it."

Aris began scanning the tables and grabbed the largest drink she could find. Another girl picked up the beverage next to hers.

The young lady had long blond hair and eyes like blue lagoons—a classic beauty. Her dress was pretty, with a modest neckline. She looked young, but Aris was sure she would become an absolutely gorgeous woman someday.

The two ladies glanced at each other before taking small sips of their drinks, savoring the taste.

"Good evening," Aris said, tucking a strand of hair behind her ear.

She gave a dazzling smile to the other girl. It was the smile she rehearsed every day in the mirror.

"Yes, good evening," the blond replied, smiling shyly. That smile didn't seem as well-practiced as Aris', but it was still rather cute. "These drinks are quite good."

Aris watched the girl drink elegantly, with the grace expected of the nobility. As she brought her glass up to her lips, she tucked a strand of her long blond hair behind her ear. She looked weak, just as Aris did.

"To tell you the truth, I haven't even had breakfast or lunch today," Aris whispered. She knew Lucine was watching her like a hawk, and she didn't dare look at food at the moment. "I barely got permission to drink this."

The younger girl sighed. "Me too. My maids found out I was going to the palace and stopped feeding me since yesterday," she lamented, gazing sadly at her drink. "I don't know why I have to deal with this." Then she glanced at Aris again. "You are Lady Aris Horissen, correct?"

"Yes," Aris replied, wondering how this girl knew her name.

"I've heard much about you from my father."

"Is that so?"

"My name is Violet d'Essel."

"Ah."

Aris' father had said that Duke Essel often spoke of how angelic and charming his daughter was. He boasted of her golden hair and how she had the bluest eyes and that she was beautiful, just like him.

She really is worth boasting about.

Aris had assumed that Louison was exaggerating his daughter's beauty, but Violet truly was stunning. While Aris was pretty, she was just another girl compared to Violet.

Thank God, Aris thought, relieved.

If she couldn't avoid the crown prince's attention, she would just have to hang around the most beautiful lady at the party. Violet was also one of the top maidens selected by the emperor to be the crown prince's bride. If His Royal Highness fancied Violet more than her, things would go just as planned.

"I've heard much about you as well, Lady Essel," Aris said.

"Please, call me Violet."

"Of course, Violet. Call me Aris."

"All right."

The two girls finished their drinks simultaneously and stared mournfully at their empty cups, as if rehearsed. Violet, noticing this, giggled, and Aris began laughing with her.

"We truly are similar," Aris said as they sat down their glasses.

"Announcing the arrival of His Royal Highness, the crown prince!" a page called out.

The star of tonight's tea party, the crown prince, had finally arrived after finishing his duties for the day. All of the young ladies who had looked as if they were on the brink of death perked up instantaneously. Determined to greet the prince and start eating, the ladies all snapped their attention toward him.

"Welcome, ladies," Hiel said.

Basking in everyone's rapt gazes, he ran his fingers through his long blond locks and thought about how his good looks were always the center of attention.

Why am I so handsome? Hiel wondered as he examined his reflection in the mirror.

His glossy blond hair cascaded down his shoulders and his blue eyes sparkled like twin lakes. His eyes were full of elegance and grace and looked more beautiful than the rarest jewels.

"Hmm."

"What's wrong, Your Royal Highness?"

"I just feel like I'm too perfect."

"But of course," his gentleman-in-waiting began, ready to sing his praises. "Your every movement is marked with elegance; you have chiseled good looks, and you're the crown prince of this empire. No man in the world could compare."

Hiel nodded in agreement, smugness permeating his face. He gave his father's list another once-over. The names of the capital's finest young ladies filled the sheet front to back, and he could tell how much effort his father had put into procuring this list.

I want to meet them all!

Some of the names on the list were unfamiliar to him, and he was shocked to learn that there were beautiful ladies in the capital that he hadn't met yet. If this was indeed true, he just had to meet these young women. He wanted to be surrounded by them and watch them praise his beauty.

"All of the preparations have been made, Your Royal Highness."

"Very well." The crown prince nodded at the attendant and took one last pleased look at his reflection. With a satisfied grin, he exited his chambers, his gentleman-in-waiting following him alongside his guards. Razaen."

"Yes, Your Royal Highness?" responded the gentleman-in-waiting.

"What are the ladies doing right now?"

"I heard that they have not been eating because they are waiting for your arrival."

"They haven't started eating yet?" Hiel asked, confused.

"To tell you the truth, ladies typically eat very little to maintain their slim figures."

"That means...!"

"They all want to look as beautiful as possible for you, Your Royal Highness."

Razaen's words put Hiel in an even better mood. It was no easy feat to endure hunger. And yet, to think that all these women were willing to go hungry for him! Such devotion!

Armed with this knowledge, Hiel decided to appear as handsome and charming as he could today. It was the least he could do for these young women who had suffered so much.

❀ ❀ ❀

The ladies were gathered in the Spring Garden. As Hiel sauntered toward them, they began turning their attention toward him, one by one.

"Welcome, ladies," Hiel said.

Ah, what a delight!

Hiel smiled kindly at each lady he saw. The ladies began drawing toward him as if he was magnetic.

"Good evening, Your Royal Highness," echoed the many noble ladies.

He could hear their high-pitched voices greeting him here and there. Their voices sounded just as beautiful as they looked. Each lady smiled at Hiel brightly, and once they had greeted him, they turned around and immediately rushed to the table of snacks they'd been eyeing since their arrival.

An interesting phenomenon was occurring, wherein the girls would say hello when Hiel walked by, and then immediately begin gorging themselves on snacks once he passed. Hiel, of course, had no idea this was happening.

"Good evening, Your Royal Highness," Aris said.

Her time with Violet had been so enjoyable that she had missed the opportunity to get her greetings to the prince out of the way. If she had really tried, she could've been one of the first to greet him. But by the time the prince approached them, he had spoken to nearly all of the attendees. Next to her, Violet greeted the crown prince as well.

I want to eat too.

Unbeknownst to Hiel, a fierce battle for food raged behind him. Every tray the maids brought to the tables was emptied in the blink of an eye. It was clear that the ladies were all starving, Aris and Violet being no exception. They just wanted to get this over with and start eating.

"Ah, and you are?!" Hiel exclaimed, stopping in front of Violet. There was no doubt that he was absolutely taken with her, as she was the most beautiful girl here. None of the other ladies could compare.

"My name is Violet d'Essel."

The crown prince nodded slowly. While he was busy appraising Violet, Aris took the opportunity to slip away.

"My lady!" Lucine yelped, hot on her heels.

"Don't try to stop me!"

Sweets! Delicious honey and chocolate! Aris desperately needed the rush of happiness and pleasure only sweets could bring her.

She felt sorry for abandoning Violet with the crown prince, but she had to satisfy her hunger first. Aris then reached out for the snacks she had been craving since she'd arrived. Her motion seemed to alert the other ladies that food was still available, and they charged toward it without hesitation.

Aris got there first and grabbed a handful before the rest of the ladies could. "Got it!"

She could finally eat now. Aris was about to take a bite when, out of nowhere, a girl ran into her, toppling them over like a pair of felled trees.

"Ahh!!!"

The cookie fell out of Aris' hand and rolled out of her sight.

"I'm sorry!" the young lady said, helping Aris stand up.

However, Aris was still in a daze.

My cookie... she whimpered.

That cookie was long gone. Holding onto a last strand of hope, she checked the tray where she found it, but to her dismay, the few cookies she had left there had already been taken. The palace maids, astonished at the pace the young ladies were eating, had started bringing out smaller amounts of snacks. They were worried about running out of food before the tea party ended if they kept bringing it out at their current rate.

"You should have paid more attention to your surroundings, Lady Aris," Lucine tutted, brushing off Aris' dress.

The brunette girl looked devastated.

"I'm so sorry!" the other lady repeated, bowing her head in embarrassment.

"No, no, it's fine."

"Still, I feel so bad..."

"I mean, it's not really fine, but it's not like you did it on purpose," Aris said reassuringly, not allowing herself to display the despair of losing her favorite snack.

Lucine smiled approvingly. "Here you go," she said, holding an assortment of sweets in her hands.

"Huh?"

"I grabbed a few of the treats you were staring at earlier."

"Lucine!"

"Yes, my lady?"

"I love you."

At last, she could eat her beloved cookies and escape from the clutches of hunger. Aris began to enthusiastically eat the snacks Lucine had saved for her. Around the room, some ladies with clever maids were doing the same. As she chewed, Aris glanced at Hiel. It seemed that he was quite besotted with Violet, as he was still by her side.

I knew he was into blondes, she thought.

Luckily for Aris, Violet was so pretty that the crown prince could barely show interest in anyone else.

Maybe I should save some snacks for her —

At the rate the ladies were plowing through the refreshments, it was almost certain that there would be none left for Violet. Her maid had likely set some snacks aside for her, but Aris was sure it wouldn't be enough for the girl. After all, Violet had gone hungry longer than Aris had.

Finally, the crown prince left Violet's side to approach other ladies for some small talk.

Violet looked visibly relieved.

"Aren't you hungry?" Aris asked, walking toward her.

Violet looked like she could cry. "I really just wanted to run away."

The young girl had assumed she would just say hello and then feast upon sweets, but that had not been the case. A frown tugged the corners of Violet's lips downward, and Aris' heart broke for the girl.

Wow, she's so pretty that her sadness looks intensified… Aris thought as she looked at Violet.

Perhaps this was the power of beauty. Violet's maid approached her with a small plate of sweets, and the girl began to eat hungrily. Aris watched her eat for a moment, then held out the cookies and chocolates that she had saved.

"It's not much, but you should eat it," she said.

"Oh my goodness!"

"I'm sure you're hungrier than I am."

Touched, Violet looked up at Aris with shining eyes. "Thank you so much."

"Not at all."

"Would it be all right if I called you Big Sister?" Violet asked.

Aris nodded. *It looks like sweets were the key to her heart,* she thought, amused. If the crown prince had known this, he might have had better luck with Violet.

"So, the crown prince really took a liking to you," Aris said.

Violet sighed loudly. "I don't like him."

"Why not?"

"He has many mistresses, and he doesn't know how to treat a lady," Violet said with a conviction far surpassing that of any normal thirteen-year-old.

Aris suddenly felt as though she'd found a kindred spirit in Violet. Now that their bellies were full, some ladies began to approach the crown prince for a chat, and Hiel welcomed them all with a charming grin.

"Aha," said Aris.

"See?"

"He really likes women," the two said at the same time.

The girls shared a look.

"I don't like him," Violet repeated.

"Me neither," Aris said, nodding.

Neither of them had the slightest interest in the crown prince. Upon discovering that their views on men were quite similar, they decided to walk to the far end of the garden to chat a bit more.

"My father always told me that a good man must always be loyal to his wife," Violet said. She had learned how to discern a good man from Duke Essel's teachings.

"I agree," Aris said.

The male lead was charismatic and incredibly talented, but he didn't have a flamboyant personality. He was just a man who cherished the woman he loved. Of course, he just so happened to be gifted with good looks and skill. Remembering that a man like that waited for her made Aris' mood lighten considerably, and she smiled as she thought about her future husband.

"I already have a man I like," Aris admitted.

Violet's eyes widened. "What kind of man is he?" she asked, eager to hear more.

"He lives on the battlefield."

The war had yet to end, so the male lead hadn't returned from the war zone at this point. He hadn't been bestowed a title yet, but the court was in agreement that he would be awarded one upon his return. Just this morning, the newspaper was filled with articles that lauded his amazing deeds. He was a hero.

"He's the one who won the recent battle against the Oraanian Empire," Aris explained.

"Ah," Violet hummed. She knew who Aris was talking about. "Are you sure? He's a commoner."

The convention was that nobles married only other members of the aristocracy. To have a lady of noble blood marry a commoner was very unusual.

Aris nodded. "I want to get to know him."

"Why don't you write a letter to him, then?"

"A letter?"

"Yes. What if you wrote a friendly letter to him and you became pen pals?" Violet suggested with a smile.

Such an excellent idea hadn't crossed Aris' mind before, but she could practically smooch Violet out of gratitude. It was so nice to find a friend who could help her out like this. She didn't have to wait for the marriage proposal to get to know her future husband, she could start right now!

"Here you are," Hiel said, making a beeline toward Violet.

Contempt flashed in her eyes, but she fixed her expression before the crown prince could notice and smiled politely at him.

"Yes, Your Royal Highness," she replied sweetly.

"Who is this next to you?"

Even though Aris had greeted him earlier, it seemed that the prince had barely noticed her presence beside Violet. Then again, she wasn't this type, so it was no surprise that he didn't remember her.

"I am Lady Aris Horissen."

After re-introducing herself, Aris curtsied politely.

Recognition dawned on the crown prince's face. "Ah, so you're Aris Horissen," he said.

"I'm surprised you know of me."

"Father told me about you. He told me about both of you, actually," he explained, looking at both Aris and Violet. So the emperor had indeed singled them out. However, Aris wouldn't just let someone else decide her fate. "You two ladies seem close," he continued.

"We have a lot in common," Violet replied.

"I see," Hiel said, smiling brightly. He turned to Aris. "You both seemed to be enjoying your conversation. I'd love to know what you were talking about."

Aris felt like Hiel was making an effort to get closer to her. She pondered over what to say for a moment before replying. "We weren't talking about much," she said.

"I'd still like to know, if you don't mind," he said, pressing the subject.

"We were talking about what we look for in a man," Aris responded honestly.

"And what is it you look for?" he asked, expecting a shower of flattery.

Hiel wanted to hear about how she had always dreamed of having a dashing prince like him come sweep her off her feet. She wasn't his type, but he needed to hear that he was her type.

"Well," Aris began, noticing the expectant look in the crown prince's eyes. Unfortunately for him, Aris wasn't in the business of doing charity. "I like men who are loyal, and will only care for one woman for the rest of their lives."

Hiel's expression immediately soured at the unexpected response. "One woman?" he asked, stunned.

"The kind of man who will only love and cherish the one woman most important to him," Aris continued coolly.

"I see," Hiel sniffed, turning on his heel to walk away.

Aris watched his retreating figure with glee.

Yes!

With this, there would be no chance of Hiel developing an interest in her. This was an excellent turn of events. Everything was going just as planned.

The flowers in the garden were in full bloom, and freesia petals floated in the air over a dazzling array of sweets and refreshing beverages.

After filling their systems with some food, the ladies finally returned to their senses and remembered the purpose of the party—getting to know the crown prince. Surrounded by gorgeous women, Hiel looked at each of their faces and smiled contentedly. Violet was still next to him, as he refused to leave her side.

A few paces away, Aris enjoyed a cup of tea by herself. She sipped slowly, savoring the delicate fragrance of the tea. The tea served in the palace had a sweeter finish than the tea she usually had.

"Is it good?" Lucine asked.

Aris nodded and continued to watch the scene unfolding before her.

"What a beautiful garden," she murmured.

The Spring Garden was truly worthy of its name. Flowers bloomed on every tree and shrub and, according to what she had heard, they remained in bloom all year round. Aris couldn't believe her eyes. The foundation of the garden was made of a magical material. It maintained the garden at a constant temperature, no matter the season. Aris wished she had a garden like this at home, where she could sit every day and drink tea.

"I brought you some more snacks, my lady," Lucine said.

"Thank you."

Aris had filled up on the sweet snacks, so she was no longer desperately hungry. She smiled peacefully as she enjoyed her tea and cookies.

"Ugh," Violet sighed, finally free from the crown prince's attention.

"Good work out there," Aris said sympathetically.

She knew Violet didn't like the crown prince, but she had to smile around him regardless. He was still the crown prince. How could she possibly disrespect the future emperor?

"What a chore," Violet grumbled, settling into the seat next to Aris. "What kind of tea is that?"

"It's freesia flower tea."

"That sounds nice, I'd like to have some too."

As her maid stepped out to get some freesia tea, Violet sighed heavily.

"The garden is so beautiful. Let's look at the flowers and cheer up," Aris offered.

Violet ground her teeth. "Oh, it's beautiful, all right. So beautiful, I want to set it all on fire," she huffed.

It seemed that dealing with Hiel for such a long time had left Violet with a lot of pent-up stress. Aris gave Violet her kindest smile, one that she'd practiced several times in the mirror. Violet seemed to soften somewhat.

"You have a very pretty smile, Big Sister," she said.

The Male Lead Is Mine

"I do?"

"If that jerk had seen you smile, I'm sure he would have been all over you."

Aris laughed at Violet's new name for the crown prince.

"Father won't be pleased," Violet mumbled.

Hiel had all but confirmed that he had chosen her as his dancing partner for the ball. At this point, everyone was expecting him to announce it soon.

"My head hurts," the younger girl said, gently massaging her temples.

Her maid returned with the tea, and Violet took a dainty sip.

Gracefully holding her teacup, she looked over at Aris. "You look so elegant when you drink tea, Big Sister," she said.

"Really?"

"Yes."

Aris had practiced very hard to look as elegant as she did, but Violet didn't need to know that.

"My etiquette instructor is just an excellent teacher," Aris said humbly.

"Oh, who is your instructor?"

"Are you interested in learning from her?"

"I don't really like my current etiquette instructor, so I was considering switching," Violet clarified.

The frown on her face revealed her dissatisfaction with her teacher. After getting the name of the instructor from Aris, Violet seemed to be seriously considering changing tutors.

A few tables from them, Hiel had attached himself to another pretty blond who also appeared to be less than thrilled at receiving his attention. He had found another victim to pester.

"It's a lot more fun being over here," Violet said, watching the two as if she was at a comedic play.

"Isn't it?" Aris laughed and drank her tea. "I had to deal with that mess earlier today too."

Violet seemed to dislike the crown prince far more than she had when the tea party first started. If Aris had been forced to entertain the crown prince, she was sure she would feel the same way.

"I love the garden, but…"

"…I hate the guy who owns it," the girls said in unison, before bursting into a fit of giggles.

At the end of the tea party, a light dinner was served. Aris and Violet quickly ate their meals and said their goodbyes, departing as soon as they could. The other ladies remained within the dining hall, wanting to spend more time with the crown prince. Hiel seemed like he wanted to have both ladies stay a while longer, but since their fathers had arrived to pick them up, he had to let them go.

Ian and Louison were glad to see their daughters becoming friends. The girls chatted cheerfully the entire way to the carriages. After promising to write to each other soon, each got into their respective carriages and headed home.

"It looks like you're good friends with Lady Essel now."

"We have a lot in common," Aris said with a smile. They shared their views on men, specifically. "Father?"

"Yes?"

"Are you ever going to get remarried?" Aris asked.

Her mother had passed away while giving birth to her, and Ian had never remarried.

One night, in a drunken stupor, he mistook a maid for his late wife. Lucine was the result of that night. If that hadn't happened, he never would have had any other children.

"Remarried? How scary," Ian murmured.

Aris fixed her Father with a serious gaze. "Really, once I get married, you'll be all alone."

"You will become Marquise Horissen," he said.

"Father!"

"I mean it. I intend to pass my title onto you." This had never happened in the original novel. Aris had been too foolish to receive any kind of title then, but things were different now. Ian considered his daughter more than worthy of the title of marquise. "That means you'll continue to live on our estate."

"Are you going to find a husband for me?"

"Yes, I will."

Aris was shocked.

Things keep straying further from the original plans, she thought.

At this rate, she'd never be able to marry the male lead.

"I don't want to become a marquise," she said.

"Aris..." Ian was confused.

Most people would kill for such a title, so he couldn't understand why his daughter was refusing it.

"Pass your title on to someone else. All I need is a little money to live on in the future."

Becoming the marquis meant she'd be tied down with obligations and duties, with no time of her own. Her future plans of living a cozy, stress-free life with the male lead would fly right out the window. Why did her father think she didn't want to become the crown princess? It was because she didn't want the responsibilities that came with the title.

"I've made myself clear, right?"

"But Aris!"

"I already said I don't want it," she emphasized.

She was sure one of her relatives would be more than happy to take over the estate. There were plenty of Horissen's living in the capital. Surely at least one of them was capable enough to become the marquis.

"I really like Lady Violet. We decided to have tea together sometime," Aris said, changing the subject quickly. Ian did not press the matter any further. "I think the crown prince liked her."

"Hmm."

"He particularly liked all of the blonde ladies."

"Just as you predicted."

"Yes," Aris said with a grin. She felt sorry for Violet, but she was just happy she'd avoided the crown prince's attention.

Once the tea party concluded, Hiel began walking toward his residence, the Lion Palace. His gentleman-in-waiting, Razaen, followed dutifully behind him.

"The ladies were all quite beautiful," Razaen said.

"There were a lot of blondes," Hiel remarked, satisfied that many of the women had been to his liking.

In his opinion, the night had been a great success. He opened the doors to his bedchambers, only to find his father waiting for him.

"The tea party went on for longer than I'd expected," Juselle said, checking the time. It was already past ten.

"Father, what brings you here?" Hiel asked.

"I'm here to hear your decision," Juselle said, prompting his son to hold his chin between his fingers. "You are aware of the purpose of tonight's party, aren't you?"

"To find a lady to dance with?"

"Correct."

"I've made up my mind," Hiel said without hesitation.

"Who have you chosen?"

"Lady Aris Horissen."

From the doorway, Razaen could hardly contain his surprise. Lady Horissen was not one of the ladies that Hiel had been so fond of. The crown prince had hardly given her a second glance at the tea party!

"I see."

"What do you think, Father?"

"You've made an excellent decision," the emperor said.

Hiel had chosen the lady that Juselle favored the most. Satisfied with his son's response, he left the room. He would have to relay the news to Marquis Horissen. As he watched his father leave, Hiel's mouth twitched into a smile.

"Why did you choose her?" Razaen asked, unable to repress his curiosity.

Hiel tossed his blond locks. "I had to choose her so my other girls wouldn't get jealous."

"Excuse me?"

"I mean, think about it. Almost every lady at that party was already head over heels for me. If I chose my dance partner amongst them, I'd surely hurt their feelings. I had no choice but to pick someone they wouldn't even consider competition."

"Ah."

"Aris Horissen isn't even interested in me. She likes another type of man. If I chose her for my first dance, she'd just be grateful for the honor. She would never assume it signaled anything romantic."

"I see!" Razaen exclaimed, stifling a laugh.

Today, like all other days, the crown prince's thoughts were full of arrogance.

"Bring me a pen and paper. I want to write a letter," Aris demanded.

"A letter?"

"Yes."

Lucine was confused, but did as she was told. The bottom of the stationery was decorated with a floral pattern, and the paper had a subtle fragrance.

"Do you think it suits me?" Aris asked.

"It does."

"Good!"

Then Aris began writing.

Dear Commander Roy,

I would like to commend you for your efforts in protecting our borders. My heart races whenever I read

of your bravery and successes. It is now spring in our Empire. I understand it is still winter where you are currently stationed. Please take care of your health. You need not write back.

"All I need to do now is send it," she murmured.

Roy was the male lead's first name. Although she knew where to mail the letter to, she had no idea who to address it to ensure Roy would receive it.

"I ought to send a messenger," she muttered.

"A messenger?" Lucine parroted.

"I need to know if he got it or not."

"Hmm." Lucine looked at the letter, conflicted. "My lady, do you know what's going to happen if you send a letter to a man you've never even met?"

"Sure I do. If a sixteen-year-old aristocrat sends a letter like this, rumors are bound to spread." Aris smiled.

"Exactly," Lucine said slowly. She wanted to be sure that Aris knew what she was getting herself into. "And you're alright with this?"

"Me? Yes." Aris smiled at Lucine brightly. "I like this man."

"My lady…"

"I like this man enough to marry him."

Before she had entered the novel and become Aris Horissen, she had been terminally ill. Cancer had spread throughout her body, rendering her bedridden at a young age. She had wanted to spend the rest of her life doing whatever she wanted, and so she began spending the majority of her days reading romance novels. She soon discovered that many of the men in those novels were scoundrels who treated women horribly. She hated bad boys. Every man she had ever dated had ended up breaking her heart. Because of that, she hated reading about men like them in her novels. One day, she happened upon this particular novel.

It wasn't very popular, but it was just what she had been looking for. It was as if someone had taken everything she wanted in a romance and written a book about it.

That was why she had to end up with the male lead; she just wanted a happy ending.

She wanted to send him a letter so that she could get to know him. She expected him to think she was just another one of his admirers since he probably had several people writing to him every day. She also expected that he would never write back to any of them.

"If you say so," Lucine sighed.

She knew there was no way to change her lady's mind once she'd made a decision. If she liked this man enough to consider marrying him, there was nothing she could do about that.

Sighing, Lucine called in a young man from outside the room and introduced him. "He's good at keeping secrets, and he knows self-defense. He should be fine for the job."

The man was nervous, mostly because Lucine had told him he'd be going on a personal errand for the young miss.

"What's your name?" Aris asked.

"My name is Hiun," the man responded quickly. His name reminded Aris of that awful crown prince.

She folded up her letter and handed it to Hiun. "Deliver this to Commander Roy," she instructed.

"Yes, my lady."

"Don't wait around for a response," she added.

Hiun nodded.

"You must keep this a secret," Lucine said gravely.

Hiun saw the icy look in her eyes and bowed his head meekly. Lucine was the young miss' personal maid, and she could make any other employee's life a living hell if she wanted to. The Horissen residence was an exceptionally pleasant place to work, and no one wanted to ruin that for themselves.

"I understand," Hiun said, leaving with the letter.

"I'm all right with him not keeping it a secret," Aris said with a giggle.

"But I'm not," Lucine huffed. "I don't understand why you need to send a letter to that man in the first place. Who cares if he's a hero? He's a commoner, and you're a noblewoman." Aris was a lady so refined and well-respected that she was being considered for the position of crown princess. Lucine believed a young woman of her position shouldn't have to send letters to some common man. "I heard he only likes women who are mute."

"Mute?"

"Yes."

Aris was already aware of this rumor, having read about it in the novel. Therefore, she knew it was just something Roy had made up to get his comrades to stop introducing him to women. Knowing the truth, Aris wasn't concerned about it at all.

"My lady!"

"Yes?"

"Are you going to write to him again?"

Aris nodded. "I will once Hiun returns. A battlefield is a busy place. I don't want him to be uncomfortable because I keep sending him letters," she said simply and got up from her seat.

High tea had ended, and now it was time for her to do her homework.

Her schedule would go back to normal tomorrow.

Neither she nor anyone else knew of the storm that would wreak havoc throughout the household later that night.

Ian had been called in for a private meeting with the emperor. Juselle, seeing the marquis enter, smiled smugly.

"The crown prince has chosen your daughter for his first dance," he informed him.

Ian's eyes widened with shock. "Why… Why did he select my daughter?"

"He was quite taken with her."

But Aris had told him that the crown prince had liked the other ladies better! Ian couldn't understand why he had chosen her, of all people.

"It seems that your daughter will debut in society earlier than expected," the emperor added. Most young ladies debuted on their seventeenth birthdays, but with the crown prince's decision, Aris was set to make her first appearance sooner. "I look forward to the ball next month."

"Your Imperial Majesty, please give this some more thought—"

"Declined," Juselle cut him off. He had no intention to change his mind. The emperor smiled serenely. "Isn't this a great honor for your household?"

Some honor! It was insanity, but there was no way that Ian could refuse a royal order.

The Male Lead Is Mine

He couldn't understand why the crown prince had chosen Aris. Just thinking of telling her about this made his heart break. When his meeting with the emperor ended, Ian trudged back to his carriage glumly.

As he got into the carriage, he began cursing himself. What kind of father couldn't even protect his daughter from an unwanted fate? That thought tortured him.

At last, the carriage had arrived at the front gates of the Horissen manor. Ian stepped out to find his daughter waiting for him at the door. Her long mahogany hair spilled over her shoulders elegantly, and her brown eyes were bright and clear.

What a lovely daughter he had.

She was so lovely that it was only natural that the crown prince would choose her. Aris had probably been the most beautiful girl at the tea party, and that was why he had chosen her.

"What's wrong, Father?" Aris asked, noticing the dark expression on Ian's face.

"The crown prince has chosen you to dance with at the ball," he said with a heavy sigh.

"What?" Aris gasped in utter disbelief. "Me?"

"Yes."

What nonsense was this? The crown prince had barely spoken to her, let alone given her a second glance. Why had he chosen her?

"Dear God," Aris breathed.

"Oh my goodness!" Lucine shrilled from beside her. "When will the ball be held?"

"In a month," Ian replied.

Lucine began calculating everything that had yet to be done. Aris would need more lessons with the dance instructor. Her first dance in front of high society would be with the crown prince; everyone would be watching! She needed a new dress, of course, and her makeup that day would have to be perfect.

Lucine could hardly contain her excitement. "One month isn't enough time!"

Aris had been chosen out of all of those excellent young ladies, and Lucine was lucky enough to serve her. She should have chastised her a little more when she'd sent that letter.

I don't want to go! Aris thought furiously.

"My lady, what kind of dress do you want to wear?"

"I don't care."

I hate the crown prince!

She didn't want to play dress-up and do her makeup. In fact, she didn't want to see that sorry excuse for a prince ever again.

The battlefield was a hellscape like no other. In order to live another day, one had to kill other men constantly. Amidst the bloodshed and terror, a hero was born, and he bravely fended off the attacks from the Oraanian Empire.

"Who goes there?" a guard asked Hiun, who had approached the postal hub.

There, people were sorting through letters and small packages.

"I have a letter for Commander Roy."

The guard eyed Hiun suspiciously. "Commander Roy?"

"Yes."

The Male Lead Is Mine

The guard's demeanor shifted. He gave a signal to two nearby guards, who grabbed Hiun by the arms and dragged him into the nearby barracks.

"What is the meaning of this!" Hiun yelped as he was pulled into the building.

"Security checkpoint. Remove your clothing," one of the guards said, releasing him.

Hiun had no idea what was going on, but he did as he was told. He stood in the middle of the barracks, completely bare. After the guards had inspected him and confirmed that he had no weapons, he was allowed to clothe himself again.

"We apologize for the intrusion," the same guard said, before all three bowed their heads curtly.

"Is something going on?"

"There have been several attempts to assassinate the commander, so we've increased security measures."

"Ah," Hiun said, understanding dawning on him. "I just need to give this to the commander."

He pulled Aris' letter out of his breast pocket. It still smelled sweet and floral, a stark contrast to the desolate battlefield.

"What is this?"

"The young lady I serve is an ardent supporter of the commander," Hiun said. There was no concept of a fangirl yet in this universe, so Aris had instructed him to say that she was just a supporter.

"Who do you serve exactly?" the guards asked.

Scented stationery was an uncommon item, as it was too expensive for most common citizens to purchase.

"Lady Aris Horissen," Hiun replied.

"Marquis Horissen's daughter?"

"Yes."

The guards glanced at each other. "We serve the commander directly. We can give the letter to him," one of them said.

"My lady says she does not need a response."

"Understood."

The guards took the letter with them and left.

I hope they give it to him, Hiun thought.

He had done everything he could; all that was left was to pray that the letter reached the commander safely.

"It doesn't make sense for him to get all the credit!"

Inside the camp's headquarters, a man was shouting heatedly. He had just been informed that the success of the latest battle would be attributed to someone who had not even participated in the operation. It was making his blood boil. The man, who had long green hair and twin blades strapped to his sides, pounded his chest angrily.

"I wouldn't stand for this if I were you!"

"Stop, Thurwin," Roy said, bringing his soldier's cries to a halt.

"But Commander Roy!"

"There's nothing I can do about it. It's the decision of the superiors."

Roy had been the one to strategize the entire war. He had given the directives for the latest mission to one of his superior generals, and, apparently, they would be given full credit for its success. The injustice of it all was enough to drive Thurwin mad.

The commander was the one who had strategized each operation, and he had also been the one who led the men into battle each time. The superior general had just watched from the safety of his tent, and now he would be receiving all of the glory.

Roy's blue eyes flashed with mild amusement as he watched Thurwin get angry in his stead. Sure, he felt robbed of his rightful credit, but getting upset wouldn't change anything. If he stood up against his superiors, that meant it was just a different kind of battle he had to fight. Too many people had it out for him at the moment anyway.

"I'm just waiting for the war to be over," he said with a shrug.

"Commander Roy…"

"I hate war."

He was a soldier, but he hated war. He was a skilled swordsman, but he hated violence. All Roy wanted to do was go home, get paid for his accomplishments, and live a quiet life. He thought it might even be nice to adopt a cat so he wouldn't get lonely. He ran a hand through his inky black hair.

There would be another meeting with the board of generals later to discuss the next course of action for tomorrow's battle with the Oraanian Empire. Roy was expected to be the center of attention. Many generals wanted to work with him, as they knew it would ensure their success. Truthfully, all they cared about was getting promoted.

"Oh, Commander." Thurwin sighed. He found Roy to be such a saint at times. If Roy had asked for all of the credit he deserved, he would have been the top-ranking general in the military already. However, he never did. He just did as he was told, and he did it well. "Well, at least you don't have any enemies."

Kkamang Kkamang

He was a commoner, but he was a soldier with exceptional strength and skills far surpassing those of any trained noble. He had many soldiers who were unwaveringly loyal to him. Many were already jealous of him, but none of the generals challenged him as all of them owed him for their promotions.

"I don't want enemies."

Roy was a powerful soldier, but that was it. If someone tried to take away his position, he would lose it instantly. He had no one in his corner with the power to support him in the face of political enemies. He was just a soldier, and he knew that better than anyone. If he wanted more for himself, he could lose everything he had now, including his life.

He just wanted a long, tranquil future.

"You're really something, Commander," Thurwin said, looking at Roy.

His long black hair was up in a sleek ponytail, and his blue eyes shone in contrast to his pale skin. He was quite striking; an uncommonly handsome man. Because of his looks, there were constant rumors that the ladies of the capital were all quite besotted with him. Occasionally, they would even send him love letters detailing their deep admiration for him.

Of course, Roy burned these letters upon reading them. He wasn't fond of getting his personal feelings involved on the job.

"Commander Roy," someone called out as a few of his soldiers entered. They were all men who had pledged loyalty to him after witnessing his strength and capability.

"What is it?"

There was still some time left until his meeting. Suddenly, Roy was struck with the fear that a crisis had happened. Much to his surprise, however, the soldiers merely handed him a letter that smelled faintly of flowers.

He hadn't expected this.

"A letter for you, sir."

"Really?" he blinked. This was the first letter he was receiving in a while.

"Who is it from this time?" Thurwin asked.

The soldiers glanced at each other before answering, "Apparently, it's from Lady Aris Horissen."

Most of the letters he received were from commoners; it was exceedingly rare for a noble to write him. Roy quickly opened the envelope. The letter was simple: it congratulated him on his successes, talked about the weather, and asked him to take care of his health. It also stated he needn't write back.

"Is this from the marquis' estate?" Thurwin asked, skimming over the letter quickly. He gasped. "Commander!"

The handwriting on the page was neat and steady. "It really must be from the marquis's daughter."

"So?" Roy asked.

"So, you should write her back!" Thurwin exclaimed, excited.

He couldn't care less if the commander never answered the other letters, but this one was from the marquis's daughter. Of course, an exception had to be made.

The Horissen's were a powerful noble family, and they were well-liked by the emperor. Not only that, but the marquis had one child, a daughter. If Roy married her, he could become a marquis himself. Thurwin, who had already thought of all of this, insisted that Roy send her a response.

"Good God, man," Roy sighed.

He had been planning on burning the letter, just as he always did. It wasn't smart to invest his emotions into anything.

He paused.

She said I didn't need to write her back.

Her words lingered in his mind. It was as if she had somehow known that he never responded to his letters.

"How interesting," he said, chuckling.

He gave the letter another look. It was evident that it had been written with care. Unlike the other missives he had received, this one expressly did not expect anything in return. It was different.

"You can't just burn something like this," Thurwin protested. He was looking at the big picture. "If things go well between you and this young lady, you can really move up in life."

"I've moved up enough," Roy grumbled.

"As if! You ought to be promoted to commander-in-chief!" Thurwin exclaimed. The position of commander-in-chief ranked higher than general; in fact, it was the highest position in the military. "It wouldn't be impossible, not with Lady Horissen by your side."

Thurwin felt giddy just imagining it, his heart racing at the thought of his commander being promoted to general, then commander-in-chief.

"You're being noisy," Roy said, ignoring Thurwin's words. He placed Aris' letter in his desk cabinet, where he usually kept the letters he got from his friends. He had never guarded a lady's letter like this before. "Nothing will come from a couple of letters."

"Oh, is that so?"

"Yes."

Roy's expectations were very low. Everyone who wrote to him was more or less the same: they wrote to him out of curiosity, but they quickly gave up when they failed to get a reply. This was exactly the outcome Roy hoped for by burning his letters. Nevertheless, he still felt a strange disappointment when the letters stopped coming. After all, he was still human.

He just assumed an immature young lady had sent him that letter out of boredom.

"How old is Lady Aris Horissen?"

"Sixteen years old," Thurwin replied.

Roy side-eyed him. "You certainly know a lot about her."

"Shouldn't everyone? Lady Horissen is rumored to be extremely beautiful. You have to keep up with at least this much to be considered a man."

She was still young. She might have sent him a letter because she could not meet boys her age. He decided to hold onto her scented letters, for now, intending to burn them all at once when she grew tired of him. Deep down, Roy didn't believe she would send him another letter. It didn't matter how noble or beautiful a woman was, he would not give in.

I don't like this, he thought sourly.

He didn't want to become some beautiful young lady's temporary plaything.

The only reason he was keeping Lady Horissen's letter was that she didn't expect a reply. Something about it made him feel at ease. Each time he reread her letter, a smile would slowly spread across his face. He felt it would be a shame to burn such a letter and used that as justification for holding onto it.

Perhaps, without realizing it, he was just looking for a scrap of comfort in this hellish war zone.

After her selection as the crown prince's dance partner, there was a dramatic change in Aris' daily life. Now she had to dance every day, with longer lessons and an even stricter version of her instructor. Her other lessons had been shortened by an hour and she was fitted for her ball gown during her free time. It took a long time to design, measure, and sew a ball gown, so Aris hired a famous dressmaker as soon as she could. The tailor measured Aris' shoulders, waist, arms, and legs, then left.

Aris was busily flipping through a dress catalog, trying to find something that caught her eye while she enjoyed some tea and snacks. She picked one and showed it to Violet, who had dropped by for a visit, asking, "How about this one?"

The dress in question had a high neckline and jewels sewn into the bodice. It looked very luxurious… and modest.

Violet took one look and shook her head. "Lucine would say no."

"Ah."

"She'd want you to pick something with a low neckline." Violet pointed out.

"You're right." Aris agreed, feeling sour.

She couldn't understand why she had to go through so much trouble just because of the crown prince. Who even cared what she wore to that ball!

"It might be the crown prince's first dance as an adult, but it's also your debut into high society, Big Sister."

"You're right."

"You should choose a dress carefully."

Already sick of looking at dresses, Aris felt the urge to walk up to the crown prince and demand to know why he had chosen her.

"By the way, Violet, I sent that letter," Aris said.

"Oh my, really?"

"My messenger took a magical horse, so the letter should get there in a month."

"Are you looking forward to a response?"

Aris grimaced at Violet's question and shook her head. "I don't think he'll reply."

"Why not?"

"I just get that feeling, you know?"

He probably received several letters just like hers. After all, she wasn't Roy's only admirer. She wondered if he ever replied to any letters from other ladies.

The answer, although she didn't know at the time, was a resounding no.

Still, there was a large possibility that her letter wouldn't even catch Roy's attention. Thus, she had to send him another one. It was the only way to ensure he understood that her feelings were true.

"I just want the crown prince's birthday to be over already," Aris whined.

"You really hate him, don't you?"

"He's not my type at all!"

"Same here."

The two girls grinned at each other as they spoke ill of the crown prince. There was a lot they had in common when it came to matters of the heart.

"My father wants to pass his title onto me in the future," Violet said.

"My goodness!"

"I said yes," Violet said. She was the type of girl who liked to take on new work. "That's why I have to choose the right man. He has to be satisfied with his current position in life."

Violet was young, but she knew her power and privilege well. That was why she had no interest in becoming the crown princess. Even Aris agreed that Violet was much better suited to be a duchess than a crown princess.

"The crown prince invited me to tea," Violet grumbled.

Aris, whom the crown prince had chosen to dance with, had not been invited to such a thing.

"I think he chooses a certain type of woman to play around with, and a different type of woman to dance with," she added.

Aris nodded at Violet's words. "That's the only explanation as to why he picked me."

It was probably for the best that he didn't choose a woman he was actually interested in. Dancing with any random young lady would start far fewer rumors than if the crown prince picked a lady he liked to be his partner. That being said, Aris didn't like that she was just any random young lady.

"I want to write my next letter already." Aris sighed.

"How long do you plan on writing to him?" Violet asked.

Aris pondered for a moment before lifting two fingers. "Two-and-a-half-years."

"Ah."

"I think that should be enough time."

After two-and-a-half years, they would be married. That was all the time she needed.

One month flew by in an instant, and the fresh spring air slowly melted into the simmering summer heat.

Quietly, Ian took out a jewelry box. Inside it was something he had planned to give to his daughter since the day she was born, but, now that the day had arrived, he couldn't believe that time had passed so fast.

"You called, Father?" Aris asked, entering the study.

Her glossy brown hair bounced with every movement. Lucine had been taking special care of Aris' hair, and it looked more lustrous than ever. Aris had also been eating less; she'd lost a bit of weight over the last month. A slender figure was in vogue at the moment, so she had conformed to the latest trends.

Ian couldn't believe the changes his daughter had gone through just to dance with a man. She looked a little unfamiliar, somehow.

"Come here," he said, and Aris approached him.

Once she had gotten close enough, Ian held out the jewelry box to her.

"This is..." Aris trailed off.

"Open it."

There was a gorgeous blue diamond inside the box. It was unbelievably large. Aris reached out and touched the diamond.

"It's the necklace your mother used to wear when she was alive. It was passed through generations of Horissen's."

"It's mine now?"

"Even if you decide not to become the marquise, you are still my direct heir. It's only right for you to have it."

Ian looked as if he was about to cry. Aris smiled at him. "Don't cry."

"There's dust in my eyes."

"It's not like I'm getting married now or anything," Aris laughed and held the necklace in her hands. The blue diamond sparkled brilliantly. She would surely be the center of attention if she wore this. "I'll wear it to the ball."

"Very well."

"I just want it to be over already. Lucine won't let me eat," Aris grumbled. She had been on a diet for a month. Lucine had been strict, telling her that she was representing all of the noble ladies in the entire empire. Aris touched her face. "Look how small my face is now!"

"You were already thin, to begin with."

"That's what I said too, but it was no use," Aris complained.

This is all because of that stupid crown prince!

She intended to step on his feet while they danced and pass it off as an accident. Being stepped on by a lady's high heel was extremely painful, so Aris had been practicing the best way to step on the crown prince's foot while she practiced the rest of her dancing at night. Everything would finally be over tomorrow. After the ball,

74

she would be free to eat all of the delicious food she wanted. She had already made plans with Violet to eat cake at a café in a few days.

Violet, she sighed silently.

Violet had gotten out of the crown prince's invitation for tea by pretending to be ill. It seemed the crown prince believed her, as he didn't press the matter, but not before he had a mountain of herbs and medicines sent to her home. She'd told Aris that she had gotten in trouble when she was caught throwing it all away.

Aris had still not received any invitations, despite having been chosen as his dance partner.

She would have declined them under the pretense of illness, anyway.

"I'm going to ask him while we're dancing."

"Ask him what?"

"Why he chose me."

Aris had a pretty good idea as to what the crown prince's reasoning was, but she wanted to hear it for herself.

The blue diamond rested atop Aris' collarbone, glittering beautifully. Aris' long chestnut hair cascaded down her back and was adorned with jewels and pins. A bracelet hung loosely from her wrist. Her dress exposed modest cleavage and accentuated her waist dramatically—all the result of the month it had taken the dress to come to life. Her makeup was subtle and sophisticated, and, in the light, she looked angelic.

She was still young, so she had decided against sultry makeup. Lucine thought she could pull it off, but Aris had been adamant. The only time she would do her makeup like that would be at her wedding.

"You look gorgeous," Lucine cooed, admiring her masterpiece.

The young lady had been on a diet longer this time, so she looked thinner and lovelier than usual. Lucine nodded in approval, satisfied with the changes to Aris' appearance.

"Do you like it?" Aris asked.

Lucine clapped her hands with delight. "You're going to be the belle of the ball tonight!"

"Yeah."

Aris just wanted to eat food after the party was over. She wondered if the crown prince knew she endured so much suffering just to dance with him for a few minutes. Actually, maybe it was better that he was unaware. She didn't want to be associated with him any longer than necessary.

All of the preparations are done.

She practiced how she would step on the crown prince's feet again. None of his toes would be safe tonight.

Ian opened the door and entered. He was at a loss for words, seeing how different his daughter looked now. The blue diamond looked beautiful on her. It was as if the necklace had elevated Aris' appearance.

"Father, what's the matter?" Aris' earrings swayed as she moved her head. They were also crafted from blue diamonds, to match the necklace she was wearing.

"You look beautiful."

"Oh, Father." She ran to Ian and looped her arm through his. "You look dashing today too."

She would be escorted to the palace by Ian today, as he had also received an invitation to the ball.

All of the ladies in attendance at the tea party had also received invitations. Apparently, the crown prince had chosen a few other ladies to dance with. Of course, his first dance would still be with Aris.

She descended the staircase to the ground floor and boarded her carriage. Lucine would follow in the carriage behind hers.

"I'm going to be with Violet once we get to the palace."

"Are you talking about Lady Essel?"

"Yes."

Once she danced with the crown prince, her job was over. Then she would go look for something to eat. She was positive Violet was thinking the same thing.

A chandelier hung heavily from the ceiling, each of its diamonds sparkling brightly. There was a beautiful tapestry hung on the walls, with a complex design embroidered into it. Aristocrats began trickling into the lavish ballroom. This ballroom was typically used for national celebrations, and, today, it would be used for the crown prince's coming-of-age ball.

The crown prince, tonight's star, had yet to arrive. Realizing this, Aris decided to circle the ballroom with her father. She quickly recognized some ladies from the tea party.

They're paying attention to me now.

They were all looking at Aris. The blue diamond around her neck was certainly attention-grabbing, but that wasn't why they were staring. They knew she was the young lady that the crown prince would dance with first.

"Everyone's looking at you, my lady."

"Yeah."

Lucine looked proud. Not only were the ladies looking Aris' way, but so were the men at the ball. Aris didn't consider herself particularly pretty, but she had a reputation for being one of the most beautiful ladies in the capital.

She didn't have dazzling looks, but there was a certain magnetism about her. Lucine always thought her young lady didn't understand just how beautiful she really was. She was glad that she'd worked so hard to doll her young lady up.

"Big Sister!"

Violet and Louison had entered the ballroom. Behind Violet was her maid, Anthe.

Anthe's eyes widened. She looked at Aris, and then at Lucine. Lucine looked at Violet, and then at Anthe. Violet and Aris both looked stunning—their dresses, makeup, and accessories were all close to perfection. However, Violet's necklace couldn't compare to Aris'.

Darn it, Anthe thought, biting her lip. It was uncommon to see a necklace with a diamond of that kind of beauty. Violet's necklace was certainly nice, but it paled in comparison to Aris' blue diamond. *We've lost this time.*

She made up her mind to win next time, determination blazing in her eyes.

We barely won, Lucine thought, silently thanking the Marquis for having gifted Aris the necklace. With it, Aris sparkled just a little brighter than Violet. *I can't let my guard down.*

The Male Lead Is Mine

Violet's maid was talented—Lucine would admit that much. She looked forward to seeing how their next meeting would play out, as did Anthe. They broke their intense eye contact and bowed their heads at each other.

They were connected by a certain camaraderie that only they knew.

"Ah, I look gorgeous as always," Hiel crooned at his reflection.

"You're absolutely correct, Your Royal Highness," his gentleman-in-waiting agreed.

"I'm sure the ladies have all come ready to impress me tonight."

"Of course, Your Royal Highness," the gentleman-in-waiting said sycophantically.

Hiel sat for a moment, soaking in the praise, then he said, "Good. Let's go, then."

It was time for the star of the show to make his grand entrance. He sauntered out of the Lion Palace, taking his time. It wouldn't take very long to get to the ballroom on foot, but Hiel decided to take his carriage anyway. "I wonder why her letter never came," he murmured.

"Letter?"

"The letter from Lady Essel."

All the other ladies had accepted his invitation to tea, each dressed beautifully just as he liked. Violet was the only one who had not come. Each of the ladies had promised to write him letters, so he had prepared elegant stationery for them to use. Violet was the only one who had not sent him a letter.

All she did was write to tell me she was sick."

"Your Royal Highness."

"I know she's interested in me."

Violet was young, but she was shockingly beautiful for someone of her age. Hiel had never seen blonde hair as luminous as hers before.

"She just doesn't know how to express her feelings because she is so young."

Hiel perked up at his gentleman-in-waiting's assurances. "That has to be the case, right?"

"Of course, Your Royal Highness."

For a moment there, he had wondered if she had been avoiding him.

"Hmm." Hiel was deep in thought.

Thinking about Violet suddenly reminded him of Aris, the lady he would be dancing with tonight. A lady with convictions as strong as Lady Horrisen's would never change, even for a man such as himself.

She's the tiresome type.

It was best to simply remain friends with her. He alighted the carriage and began walking toward the ballroom.

"Announcing the arrival of His Royal Majesty, the crown prince!"

The star had arrived.

Hiel entered the ballroom, and everyone immediately turned to look at him. He walked in alone, making a grand entrance. His long golden hair hung freely, and his blue eyes sparkled.

He's good-looking, I'll give him that, Aris thought, downing her drink.

Lucine had allowed her to have a beverage before she danced. Violet had also received permission from her maid and was sipping her drink slowly.

As Hiel walked further into the ballroom, young ladies began flocking to his side. It seemed that beautiful women would always surround beautiful men, no matter what they did. A pleased smile tugged the corners of Hiel's lips upwards; he was enjoying everything about the moment.

One by one, he began greeting each of the ladies that had approached him.

"Father," Aris said, looking at Ian.

"Yes."

Now that the crown prince had arrived, it was only natural to go greet him. Violet looked uneasy, remembering how Hiel had behaved at the tea party.

"Violet, let's go," Duke Essel said.

"Yes, Father."

However, she couldn't always be true to her emotions. The crown prince was the future emperor of Xenon, and he was the star of tonight's ball. It was only proper to greet him.

Aris and Violet were displeased but still began walking towards Hiel.

"Oh." Hiel's eyes twinkled at the sight of Violet before noticing that she was with Aris again.

"Happy birthday, Your Royal Highness."

"Congratulations."

The girls curtsied deeply, and, behind them, Ian and Louison bowed.

"Yes, thank you."

As soon as they had finished with their pleasantries, the four swiftly moved out of the way. There were still plenty of people waiting to speak to the crown prince. Since there were so many guests, Hiel could not speak to Louison and Ian any longer. Violet and Aris visibly brightened knowing they wouldn't have to deal with the arrogant crown prince, for now at least.

"Announcing the arrival of His Imperial Majesty, the emperor!"

Everyone bowed deeply to the emperor as he entered.

He approached the crown prince and clapped a hand onto his shoulder. "Crown Prince, congratulations on becoming an adult."

"Thank you, Father."

Juselle turned and grandly addressed the attendees of the ball. "I hope you all enjoy your time tonight," he said.

Everyone began approaching to greet the emperor. The upper nobility was allowed to pay their respects first. Ian and Louison greeted the emperor with their daughters. It was Aris' first time meeting the emperor.

Juselle looked at her and said, "And you must be Lady Aris Horissen?"

"Yes, Your Imperial Majesty."

"You are just as beautiful as I've heard."

She had common brown hair and eyes but still outshined the other ladies at the ball. Violet was obviously gorgeous, but Aris was just as charming.

Aris bowed her head at Juselle's praise. "Thank you, Your Imperial Majesty."

The emperor had spoken to her because of the crown prince. This was bad news. It would be a disaster if he commanded her to become the crown princess.

I wonder if my letter arrived safely, Aris wondered. *Hiun was due to return any day now.*

Aris thought of Roy as she looked at the emperor. She had never seen his face, and she'd only ever read about him. However, the more she had to be around Hiel, the more she came to appreciate Roy.

As everyone finished greeting Juselle, music began filling the ballroom. It was finally time.

How long had she suffered, just for this moment? Aris glared at Hiel. As he approached her with a smile, she wanted to wipe the smug expression off of his face.

"Lady Essel," he said, looking at Violet. "I'll be dancing with you next."

"Yes, Your Royal Highness," Violet nodded. "Break a leg, Big Sister."

"I will."

Aris gently accepted Hiel's hand and walked to the center of the dance floor. Just as she was taught, Aris soon began dancing, Hiel matching her movements.

The time had come.

"Oh, my!" Just as practiced, she stepped firmly onto Hiel's feet. "I'm so sorry!"

Hiel furrowed his eyebrows but continued to dance. "Don't worry about it."

Hiel didn't say anything about Aris pretending to be a poor dancer, but he glared at her when she stepped on his feet a second time.

I should stop now.

She had only trampled his toes to exact petty revenge, but she didn't want to get on his bad side. Aris feigned an apologetic demeanor and bowed her head as they danced.

"You're a good dancer."

Of course she was! She had practiced for a month. She flashed her practiced smile that Violet admired so much.

"Thank you. I was so nervous at the beginning that I messed up."

"I see."

"By the way, Your Royal Highness."

"What is it?"

"Why me?" Aris asked, finally letting her curiosity get the best of her.

Hiel swept her across the dance floor and turned her in his arms. They had almost reached the end of their dance. If she didn't ask him now, she'd never know the answer.

Why did he choose her if he didn't like her?

"Because I felt like you wouldn't like me."

"Your Royal Highness..."

"That's why I chose you. Everyone else makes a big deal out of this kind of thing," the crown prince responded honestly.

"Ah."

He had just needed a girl who would leave him as soon as the dance was over.

No doubt about it, she mused.

If the crown prince had chosen to dance with a lady he liked, she surely would have thought it to be a big deal. He had chosen Aris to avoid that from happening. Perhaps he was cleverer than she had originally thought. Nevertheless, the fact that she had to suffer for a month just for his convenience still made her angry.

But at least I got my revenge.

She had stepped on him twice, and that was enough for her. It probably hurt quite a bit, considering she was wearing high heels. She'd noticed that Hiel had moved more carefully after that.

"Your Royal Highness," she said to get his attention.

He would soon leave her to ask Violet to dance. Before that, she had something to tell him.

"What is it?"

"Violet is just like me." She didn't know if he would believe her, but it was worth a shot. "Like me, she wants a man who will be loyal to her and only her."

Aris hoped this would be enough for the crown prince to let go of Violet. She had too much potential to be cooped up in the palace forever. If Violet had wanted to become crown princess, Aris would have supported her, but Violet had no interest in the title.

Perhaps Aris was being insolent, she wasn't sure, but she still said, "Don't trap a girl of only thirteen."

Hiel's face reddened as he understood the intention behind her words. "It's not any of your business."

"I'm telling you this for your sake, Your Royal Highness."

"For my sake?"

"Lady Essel wishes to become a duchess, not a crown princess. Do you think she would do anything she didn't want to do?"

At that moment, the music came to an end, and Hiel looked at Aris. He could see that there was no deceit or malice in her eyes.

"You're not lying," he said.

Aris was telling the truth. He turned around and headed towards Violet for the next dance. Violet was still young and was not quite used to wearing high heels. If she walked too much, her feet would begin to ache terribly. Aris knew she would certainly head to the powder room to rest after her dance, so she decided to head there first and wait for Violet.

A few moments later, Violet came walking in. "Big Sister, what did you tell him?" she asked.

"Mm... the truth."

Violet sat down next to her with a happy grin. "He said he would expect great things from me when I become duchess."

"Ah."

"It looks like he won't bother me anymore."

"The crown prince isn't such a fool after all."

"You're right."

Aris hadn't expected her words to reach him, but it seemed like he had given them serious thought. He was arrogant, but he could change. Maybe he had simply been moved by Aris' sincerity.

"My feet hurt." Violet kicked off her high heels with a sigh of relief. "I'm going to eat so much cake at the café," she said with a big smile.

Aris was looking forward to it as well. It would be her first time going around the capital with a friend.

"I'm going to use the restroom," she said.

"All right."

Aris rose from her seat and left the powder room. As she examined her reflection in the restroom, she noticed that some of her makeup had rubbed off.

I should ask Lucine to touch it up for me.

She washed her hands and exited the powder room, but, to her surprise, she found Hiel standing before her. "Your Royal Highness."

"I was waiting for you."

Aris gave the crown prince a strange look. Their dance had finished, so what business did he have with her now?

"You're the kind of lady who knows how to stand up for her friends."

"Thank you."

"I have plenty of women anyway. It doesn't matter if I don't have one more," the crown prince said, with a hint of regret in his eyes. It didn't matter anymore, though. All that mattered was that he didn't bother Violet. Aris found that she didn't dislike the crown prince as much as she used to. "I rather like you."

"Pardon?"

"What do you think about becoming the crown princess? Really," Hiel said.

"Where is this even coming from?"

"I need someone honest like you by my side. And also, I feel like you wouldn't get jealous if I met other women."

This jerk seemed to have arrived at a gross misinterpretation.

"I decline," Aris said firmly.

She could dance with the crown prince as many times as necessary, but she would never become his bride.

"Is that so?" Hiel asked, laughing. "I knew you would say that."

"Your Royal Highness."

"Let's be friends, then."

Violet was enough for her. It was strange that the crown prince would even want to be friends.

"I'll invite you to tea sometime. Don't pretend to be sick. I want you to come," Hiel said, before turning on his heel and disappearing into the crowd.

He was off to find more ladies to dance with.

Aris re-entered the powder room and found Violet still waiting for her. It appeared Anthe had allowed her to eat after dancing, as the little blond was happily nibbling on snacks. Next to her, Lucine was holding a plate of sweets.

"You're back, my lady."

"Yes."

"Your makeup is smudged." Lucine took out a small tin of powder and began reapplying it on Aris' face. She examined her handiwork and smiled. "There, beautiful again."

"Are these snacks for me?"

"Of course they are."

Lucine certainly knew how to keep a girl happy. Even though she was strict about food when Aris was dieting, she also knew when to reward her with delicious food. She had set aside all of Aris' favorite snacks to enjoy at the ball.

"They're tasty." Aris munched on her cookies and looked at Violet. "About the crown prince," she began.

"Yes."

"He asked if I wanted to become the crown princess."

Lucine's eyes practically bulged out of her head, and Violet's jaw dropped, forming a perfect 'O. Lucine's heart raced with excitement, though she knew not to expect anything. After all, her young lady had no intention of becoming the crown princess.

"I said no, so he said we should be friends."

"Oh my goodness," Violet said, surprised. She hadn't expected the crown prince to say something like that. "He's a good judge of character."

Aris was still slightly worried. Aris had, at one point, considered fleeing the country to escape the arrogant, womanizing crown prince. However, she'd learned today that while he was indeed arrogant, he also knew when to listen to the words of others.

"I thought I was going to have to move to another country," Violet said, echoing her thoughts.

Aris sat down next to her and sighed. "He told me not to pretend I'm too ill to attend his tea parties."

"Oh my goodness." Violet's face flushed pink. "Do you think he knew I was lying?"

"Who knows?"

Who could possibly read that strange prince? Aris shrugged and reached for another cookie, but she had run out. Lucine, realizing that Aris still had time to dance at the ball, whisked her back to the ballroom. All the men quickly took note of Aris' reappearance. They all recognized the young lady who had danced with the crown prince.

Some men who had yet to find dance partners approached her, but Aris stood in the corner by herself. She had no intention of dancing now that she had danced with the crown prince.

"My lady."

"Yes."

Lucine, standing by Aris' side, asked, "Are there any men who catch your eye?"

Today was the crown prince's coming-of-age ball, and as such, there were several high-profile guests in attendance.

"No, they're not my type," Aris said and sat down.

She didn't enjoy balls very much. Aris felt it unnecessary to look for her future husband here.

She was bored.

The battle had begun. Raids from the Oraanian Empire had disrupted the troops' formations, but this had been expected. Roy had suggested splitting their troops into two groups in anticipation of raids, and this suggestion had proven to be the correct decision.

One group would deal with the raiders, and the other group would head to the Oraanian military camp. They would need a decisive victory there.

The new general of the enemy troops was rumored to be a highly impatient man, and the Oraanian soldiers all charged in the same direction. Their mission was to take down one man, and one man only. Thurwin, wielding his twin swords, ran toward a soldier and slit his throat. Blood spurted from the wound like a fountain.

"Damn it," Thurwin spat. He should have eaten a bigger breakfast. Looking at the corpse before him, he suddenly felt pangs of hunger. He was quickly running out of strength. "I hope the other brigade gets to the camp safely."

In the center of the pandemonium stood a lonely figure. Roy was acting as bait for this battle. He had been ordered to fend off the enemy soldiers until the other Xenonian brigade set fire to the Oraanian camp.

It was a decent plan. They only had to sacrifice one of their soldiers to ensure that the enemy camp was completely wiped out. However, it seemed ironic that Roy had been chosen to become the sacrifice.

"Commander, are you alright?" Thurwin asked.

Roy nodded. "I'll survive."

The other brigade would soon return after setting fire to the camp. He just had to put up a good enough fight until then. But what if they failed and never returned? What if they had succeeded, but, fearing for their lives, chose not to return to the battlefield?

Roy smiled to himself, though it looked more like he was baring his teeth. He swung his sword. Charging forward on his horse, he slit the throats of every enemy who stood in his way. The surrounding soldiers backed away in surprise. They had known that he was a skilled swordsman, but they were not aware of how powerful his magic was.

From a distance, he could see more enemies approaching.

I don't want to die yet.

He had stayed alive in the face of great danger. Someone had sent him to the battlefield in the hopes that he would die, but he had stayed alive. He had stayed alive in places far more dangerous than here. He would survive, no matter what it took, and he'd return home.

There was no one waiting for him when he returned to Xenon. He had no pretty fiancée waiting for him at home. Even so, Roy was not ready to die. He had no particular reason to live, but he wanted to stay alive anyway.

Roy looked at the enemy general. He laughed bitterly to himself and cut down the soldiers who surrounded him in one fell swoop. Then he heard it.

"Die, Roy!" the general shouted, as he charged toward him.

It'll all be over now.

Their blades clashed against each other a few times, but the general was no match for Roy. In mere seconds, Roy had sliced the general's head clean off his body. He knew that the enemy troops would begin to fall apart once they lost a high-ranking leader like this one. The general had been waiting for Roy to attack him, but he'd grown impatient and had gone to him instead.

"Your leader is dead!" Roy roared, holding up the head of the general.

The enemy soldiers began to hesitate.

"Commander!" Thurwin shouted. "Backup has arrived!"

"Good."

Thankfully, the other brigade had returned. They had succeeded in setting fire to the enemy camp, and now they had come back for Roy. The enemy soldiers hadn't expected more Xenonian troops to arrive, and Roy could sense their confusion.

"Pull back!" one of the enemy soldiers shouted, leading the rest of the soldiers to retreat into the distance.

Thurwin watched the surviving Oraanian soldiers disappear, and let out a mighty shout.

"We have the head of the enemy's general," he bellowed. "Long live Commander Roy!"

All of the men began cheering and shouting. Roy's bravery in battle was reason enough for him to be hailed a hero. He listened to the men whooping, and slowly nudged his horse forward. The blood of the men he'd slain was splattered all over his body. It had splashed onto his face as well.

"I want to take a bath," he mumbled, still holding the head of the general.

No matter how much he was exposed to it, he could never get used to the smell of the blood. Everything about it disgusted him.

A warm breeze blew lightly. Spring would arrive here as surely as it did everywhere else. But, in this place, there was no spring. There existed only death. Roy led his horse back quietly, knowing he had only narrowly escaped death again.

There were flowers printed on the envelope again. Roy, who had just emerged from his bath, quickly snatched up the letter that had been left at his desk. It was from Lady Horissen. A sweet fragrance wafted from the stationary as if it was sprayed with perfume.

"Oh, Commander! There was another letter for you."

"I see."

"I think it was delivered through a messenger," Thurwin continued cheerfully. He liked it when Aris sent letters. "Commander, have you ever seen Lady Horissen's portrait?"

"I haven't," Roy admitted.

He had neither a reason nor the means to learn of Aris' appearance.

Thurwin quickly left the room—he had saved something to show the commander, and now was a perfect time.

Roy watched him leave, before unfolding the letter.

To Sir Roy,

She hadn't addressed him as Commander this time. He was simply Sir Roy.

The weather is quite warm in our country now. A while ago, I attended a ball in honor of the crown prince's birthday. Somehow, I ended up being selected as his first dance partner. I didn't want to but had no choice as it was ordered by royal decree. As I danced, I stepped on the crown prince's toes. I did it on purpose. I must admit, it felt rather good. Ah! Please don't let anyone know I said that. I'd like to live a long, happy life, you know.

Roy let out a chuckle as he read her amusing recounting of the birthday ball. She was a noblewoman who dared step on the feet of the crown prince that she didn't wish to dance with. He'd assumed she was yet another quiet, obedient young lady, but it seemed he had underestimated her.

"Commander!" Thurwin cried, bursting in with a newspaper. He held out the front page, which showed a large drawing of a beautiful young lady, with brown hair and brown eyes, dancing with the crown prince. "Take a look at this!"

"What am I looking at?"

"That is Lady Horissen."

"Ah?"

Roy looked back and forth between the letter and the drawing. She was but of the tender age of sixteen, but the drawing showed a maturity that could pass for nineteen.

"Isn't she gorgeous?"

"She's very pretty."

"That's all you have to say?"

"She'll stop writing me letters soon anyway," Roy said, returning to read the rest of the letter.

Hmm. Since I've revealed one of my deepest secrets today, please burn this letter after you've read it! You needn't write back.

He pictured her ending her letter with a smile. Roy could practically feel her emotions emanating through the pages. However, he was somewhat troubled by her asking to burn the letter. After a short deliberation, he eventually honored her request and tossed it into the fire, save for the envelope, which he gingerly placed into his letter cabinet.

"I can't believe you're receiving perfumed letters," Thurwin said, envy coloring his tone.

"I wonder how long this will continue."

"What?"

"These letters. How long do you think they'll keep coming?"

Thurwin had no response to the commander's question. The longest anyone had ever sent him letters had been for a period of six months. After that, the letters stopped coming.

"Today's letter could be the last," Roy muttered.

"I suppose so," Thurwin answered hesitantly.

"If the letters come for more than half a year, then I'll respond."

His gaze fell back to the newspaper Thurwin had brought. The drawing was so realistic—it was almost as if Aris was right before his eyes, smiling at him. He imagined how beautiful that smile must be in person. Roy chuckled and shook his head at these thoughts.

Aris' letters were always kind and brought him comfort, and he found himself looking forward to the next one—but that was the extent of his feelings toward her. Not only was she six years his junior, but she was also a young lady that had danced with the crown prince. She wasn't meant for someone like him. It would be dangerous for his feelings to develop any further than this. The battlefield was a lonely place, and it was only natural to want someone to lean on. He told himself he could cut her off in an instant if needed, but he felt great reluctance toward burning her letters—that was how comforting and addicting they were to him. Finding his thoughts increasingly complicated, he quickly flipped the newspaper over.

"Take this back now."

"Jeez, Commander. What kind of reaction is that?"

"She's very lovely."

"Sure, sure." Thurwin sighed, dissatisfied at the commander's lukewarm response.

He collected his newspaper and left.

Finally alone, Roy let out a sigh and looked at his hands. If he had attended that ball, could he have danced with her? Could he have held her hands and led her across the dance floor? Maybe so. Roy could only laugh at the foolish ideas the letters roused in him.

What a useless thing to think.

Lady Aris probably had no idea he felt this way. There was no way for her to know. There was no need for her to know either.

The Male Lead Is Mine

FLOWER OF THE HUNT

The flowers had bloomed beautifully. Aris had been busy arranging them into a bouquet when suddenly she turned around to face Lucine.

"What do you think of these flowers?"

"You're going to send this to him too?"

"Yes."

Aris had already sent a second letter to Roy. When she found out Hiun had been subjected to a security search, she burst out in laughter. Thinking it might be too much to ask of Hiun to deliver another letter so soon, she had sent someone else instead and decided to have the couriers switch between future deliveries. Her latest letter had also included a request for Roy to burn it after reading, but secretly she hoped he felt at least some hesitation before he'd done so.

This time, she intended to send flowers along with the letter. Since they'd likely wither before they reached their destination, she thought of having the flower petals pressed.

"He might not even be receiving your letters."

"You think so?" Aris looked dismayed.

"It's possible. You heard they inspect all the letters!" Lucine sighed, looking at her curiously. "I don't understand why you insist on continuing."

There were plenty of men in the capital, so why choose one that lived on the battlefield? She couldn't understand the young lady. If she were Aris, she would choose a far better man.

"Well, I want to send the letters anyway," Aris replied, smiling. She continued picking flowers cheerfully.

Lucine let out a dejected sigh. "Finish up quickly, then. Lady Violet will arrive any moment now."

"Ah, it's already time?"

"Of course."

It was the weekend, and Aris had no classes to fill up her schedule. Instead, Violet and Aris had planned to eat cake together at a café, even though they were probably still tired from the ball a couple of days ago. She had to finish the bouquet before Violet arrived. Aris picked her favorite flowers as quickly as she could, making sure each one smelled strong enough to be dried and treated with magic.

In a flash, she had assembled a bouquet, though admittedly, it wasn't all that aesthetically pleasing. She wondered if she should even bother sending it, but felt that she had spent too much time on it for the bouquet to go to waste. Aris quickly handed the flowers over to a maid, who accepted the bouquet and headed off to the florist's shop where the bouquet would be dried. Lucine watched the maid leave before glancing at the clock—there was only an hour left before Violet arrived.

"I'm hungry."

"Of course, you haven't had breakfast, after all."

"I need to eat as much as I can at the café. You haven't eaten either."

Lucine blushed. "Well, I need to save room for the cake…"

Lucine, along with Anthe, Violet's maid, would accompany the girls to the cake café.

"Exactly."

"About Anthe, my lady."

"Yes?"

"I think she's extremely talented." Lucine was rather looking forward to conversing with Anthe later. Of course, they shared a friendly rivalry to see who could dress their lady best, but the girls also had much more in common.

"I haven't heard you compliment someone in a while, Lucine."

"Is that so?"

"Yes," Aris said. Lucine was stern, and she had exceedingly high standards. Yet here she was, complimenting Anthe. "Lady Violet is so beautiful. She's always well-dressed, and her hair is impeccable."

"Yes, but you're the face of high society, my lady," Lucine said.

Violet was at the center of high society's fashion scene, but Aris could hold her own against her.

"You think so?"

"Yes!"

The Male Lead Is Mine

The day after she danced with the crown prince, Aris' face had been plastered on every newspaper across the empire—they called her the crown prince's chosen lady. Violet had also been mentioned, but only Aris had her picture in the newspapers. Some articles even suggested that the crown prince had fallen in love with her after their first dance. Aris seemed to be the only one unaware of her newfound popularity. Invitations and calling cards had come pouring in after the ball, but Aris had declined them all, saying she had to study. Many fine young gentlemen had also requested to meet with her, and Lucine thought it a great shame that Aris had rejected them all. Now that her lady was the shining star of the social scene, Lucine recognized it was her job to ensure Aris always looked beautiful.

"Sit down."

Aris took a seat at her vanity and closed her eyes. Lucine called in another maid, who went to task delicately applying makeup onto Aris' face. Lucine had specifically hired this maid, who was skilled in makeup for Aris. The makeup color scheme was selected to complement the dress Aris would be wearing later that day, and the maid went about deepening the contours of Aris' face.

"Open your eyes now."

"Alright." Aris' eyes fluttered open at Lucine's command.

Her reflection looked lovely, even more so than usual. She didn't look as breathtaking as she did on the day of the ball, but she still looked elegant and put together.

"You should get a massage too."

"That kind of thing is only needed when I go to the palace."

"Lady Violet might have gotten one."

"Why are you suddenly so wary of Violet?"

"I have to be," Lucine replied as if it was obvious.

Violet was a natural beauty. If Aris was to be noticed when she was with her, she must dress up. Lucine wouldn't let her young lady be outshined by anyone.

"We're just spending time together."

"You don't know what it's like to be a maid, my lady."

Lucine was right.

The makeup made Aris' eyelashes look exceptionally long and fluttery. Lucine studied her face carefully and made a few final adjustments to her look.

"I think the maid's makeup skills have improved."

"Of course she has."

After the ball, Lucine had instructed the maid to learn more about makeup for the young lady. Ian had paid for all the maid's supplementary makeup lessons, of course.

Lucine had convinced him that Aris needed to have her makeup professionally done. Now that she was in the newspapers, she had to look exquisite every time she made a public outing. Aris understood this as well.

"You and father are both really amazing."

"Really?"

"Yes, really," Aris said, rising from her seat.

The weather was warmer that day, so she slipped into a sleeveless dress and waited for Violet to arrive.

It's too bad they don't wear shorts in this world…

The coolest item of clothing available to her was a sleeveless dress. No matter how low-cut the neckline, women simply did not expose any skin from the knees up. Aris thought it was a shame mini-skirts didn't exist in this world. Maybe she could start a new trend while she was here.

Should I just make some myself? Whatever, at least I don't have to wear a corset.

Aris quickly shook off the thought, silently thankful that corsets did not exist in this universe. Otherwise, she'd surely suffer.

As Aris was lost in her thoughts, a maid knocked and opened the door.

"Lady Violet has arrived," she announced.

Aris went down to the ground floor. There was a carriage stopped in front of the manor, and as she approached it, a footman opened the door for her. Anthe and Violet, who looked pretty as ever, were seated inside.

"Long time no see," Aris grinned, Lucine climbing inside after her.

Lucine immediately began appraising Violet's outfit. She was wearing a pink sleeveless dress—modest and appropriate for a lady as young as she was. The dress was adorable. She looked fresh and playful, and her makeup was subtle and accentuated her youthful features.

She looked perfect for a girl of her age.

As Lucine was assessing Violet, Anthe, too, began scrutinizing Aris' ensemble. Aris was dressed in a yellow sleeveless gown, which complemented her shining brown hair and wide, dark eyes. Her makeup appeared simple and effortless, making her look like a truly sophisticated lady. There was a certain alluring quality about her. Anthe was deeply impressed by Lucine's skills.

"Long time no see, Big Sister!" The two ladies clasped each other's hands excitedly, completely unaware of the silent war raging between their maids. "It was so hard to get a reservation," Violet continued. She had been in charge of the reservations, as the day's outing had been her idea.

"Really?"

"All the tables were filled because it was a weekend, but luckily, one freed up! Not to mention, strawberries are in season, so they'll be offering a special strawberry cake today too!"

"How serendipitous!" Aris exclaimed. Strawberries were one of Aris' favorite fruits. She clapped her hands together with delight. "That sounds delicious."

"By the way, Big Sister, has anything happened lately?"

Aris sighed. "After rumors spread that I was the crown prince's woman, I received a mountain of calling cards. Writing personalized letters to decline their invitations took such a long time."

"Oh my," Violet sympathized. "You should have accepted a few that interested you."

"Nothing stood out to me in particular."

Violet nodded in understanding. Aris didn't enjoy balls or social gatherings, nor did she like showing off her popularity. All she needed was a pleasant view, a friend to chat with, and a cup of tea.

"I received some invitations as well."

"Really?"

"I think I'll attend a few," Violet said with a shrug.

Violet, by comparison, was far more social than Aris and enjoyed meeting new people. She enjoyed listening to the conversations and broadening her understanding of the world in this way.

"It's a good idea for you to make some appearances since you'll be the duchess in the future."

"Won't you become the marquise, Big Sister?"

"Absolutely not!"

She would be so much busier if she were to succeed as a marquise. Aris aimed to live a peaceful, relaxing life. She would fulfill her basic duties, but had no interest in doing any more than that.

The carriage pulled into a large street. Aris, who had been looking out the window, spotted the café the two were heading to.

Aris pointed. "The cake café is right over there."

"It is indeed."

The carriage came to a stop in front of the café, and Aris and Violet both exited the carriage. Aris surveyed the storefront—the door was locked, likely because of the store being on their lunch break. A line of eager customers had already formed at the door. It wasn't long before the crowd's attention became fixed on the two ladies. Most were staring at Aris, who had been recognized instantly.

"The marquis' daughter!"

"And the young lady next to her?"

"That's Duke Essel's daughter!"

"Oh, I see."

The crowd murmured and whispered at the ladies' arrival. Aris' cheeks flushed—she hadn't expected so much interest.

"I think I'll always need to wear makeup when I go on outings with you, Big Sister. Everyone is looking at us!"

Aris was at a loss. "Oh, Violet."

Lucine had been right; it would've been disastrous if she'd come out looking as she usually did.

"See, my lady? You are the face of the House of the Marquis," Lucine whispered from behind her.

Aris silently held up her thumb. "You're the best."

Having praised Lucine, Aris took Violet's hand and headed to the back of the line. It wasn't long before the café reopened and everyone began shuffling in.

I'm so excited!

Finally, she could have cake. Today, she was going to indulge to her heart's content! She couldn't wait to take a bite of that strawberry cake.

In the summer, one finds it difficult to move because of the sweltering heat, and in the winter, one finds it difficult to move because of the bitter cold. Taking this into consideration, the Empire of Xenon always hosted the annual Great Hunt in between spring and summer. Today, a conference was being held to discuss this year's hunt. It was always held in the same location, so that was never an issue. The topic of discussion was the prize for the winner of the Great Hunt, as well as the selection criteria for all the hunters who wished to participate. The most important decision, however, was the selection of the Flowers of the Hunt.

After the hunt, there was always a celebratory ball, where the winner could dance with a young man or woman of their choosing, also known as Flowers of the Hunt. If beautiful young ladies from noble households and handsome young men attended as Flowers, more people would compete, hoping to dance with them. The emperor was looking expectantly at Ian.

Ian coughed. "I decline."

"I haven't even said anything yet," Juselle grumbled.

"It is clear what you are about to say. My daughter is too young to attend the Great Hunt," Ian retorted.

Aris Horissen was the talk of the capital lately. After all, she had been the lady that the crown prince had chosen for his first dance. She was both beautiful and noble, as well as blessed with a sweet temperament. She was impossible not to pay attention to.

"How can you keep your daughter from attending?!" Juselle snapped.

He thought Ian was being unreasonable. Ian always supported him in politics or other matters of the law, but when his daughter was involved, he was unrelenting. Juselle was at a loss for words.

As soon as Ian had mustered up the nerve to disobey him, so did the other noblemen. They were all fiercely protective of their daughters. Everyone began declaring that their daughters also could not attend the Great Hunt.

"Denied! All of your daughters are required to attend!" Juselle ordered.

A dark shadow cast itself over everyone's faces. They sighed, knowing that they had lost to the emperor's absolute power. Amongst them, Duke Louison d'Essel had been the only noble to remain silent. Juselle had expected him to refuse as well, but he had not uttered a word.

"Duke Essel."

"Yes, Your Imperial Majesty," Louison said.

"You're unusually quiet today," Juselle said suspiciously.

Louison chuckled quietly and cleared his throat, "My daughter has learned how to hunt."

"So?" Juselle didn't understand what Louison was alluding to.

"She will participate in the hunt herself," Louison stated.

Violet would be there, but as a huntress, not as a Flower of the Hunt. The emperor was taken aback—the young lady was only thirteen, and a fragile lady such as herself did not suit the rugged nature of the hunt. Everyone looked at Louison in disbelief that he had discovered a loophole in the emperor's orders.

"I look forward to seeing her there," Juselle conceded.

It was uncommon for women to participate in the Great Hunt, but it happened occasionally. There had seldom been a female winner of the hunt, as most women in the empire did not receive weapons training.

"She just hunts for the fun of it," Louison said humbly, but secretly felt prouder of his daughter than ever. He had no idea that letting her learn how to use weapons would pay off like this.

"Has Lady Horissen learned how to hunt?" Juselle asked, turning towards Ian.

Ian shook his head. "No, Your Imperial Majesty."

"Then it's settled. Every young lady who attended the crown prince's ball must be in attendance at the hunt."

Juselle invited a few more ladies of his choosing.

Ian looked at Louison with envy, deeply regretting that he had not taught Aris how to fight or hunt.

As soon as the girls walked into the store, they were met with a mountain of cake stacked on the tables. The cakes were cut into small slices, with strawberries resting atop them. In the back, there were pitchers of strawberry juice, along with bowls of strawberry salad. Aris had thought that the café only served cake, but they actually had a much wider selection available.

Lucine and Anthe went to look for their table, and Aris and Violet began filling their plates with food. They each selected a few slices of cake and picked up a glass of strawberry juice. There was an assortment of cake flavors, including chocolate, crème chantilly, and cheesecake.

"There are so many kinds of cake," Aris exclaimed.

She decided to try one of each and would come back for second helpings of her favorite cake. While Aris had chosen a variety of flavors, Violet had only chosen the crème chantilly cake.

"I like crème chantilly."

"You said you've been here before, right, Violet?"

"Yes, I tried the other flavors the last time I came."

Of all the cakes she'd tried, she liked the crème chantilly best. Aris grabbed another slice of crème chantilly — she trusted Violet's taste.

The girls finished their selections and returned to their table. It was Lucine and Anthe's turn to get cake. The two maids had bonded in no time, and happily chatted away as they went to fill their plates.

"When my young lady was thirteen, she wore this brand."

"Really?"

"The fabrics and designs were quite luxurious."

"Oh my, I'll have to check it out myself."

Lucine was telling Anthe about all the clothes Aris had worn when she was Violet's age. Anthe seized the opportunity to learn as much as she could from the other girl.

When Violet turned fourteen, she would have to change her style. Thanks to the ball, she had already debuted in high society, so she couldn't be seen wearing just anything. Lucine's tips would be indispensable to Anthe.

"Lady Essel's dresses have always looked so lovely, though."

"The dressmaker we buy from specializes in dainty styles."

"Which dressmaker?"

Aris was still only sixteen. She was at an age where she could still pull off cutesy dresses. Lucine wanted to dress her up like that while she still could. Anthe told her the name of the shop, and Lucine made a mental note of it. The two exchanged tips and tricks as they filled their plates with cake.

Both considered it to be a productive day.

The crème chantilly cake was delicious —Aris could understand why Violet had only selected this cake. Soon, Lucine came by with a plate of strawberry salad. The girls alternated between bites of cake, sips of strawberry juice, and forkfuls of salad. The strawberries were fresh, juicy, and pleasing to eat.

"What do you think?" Violet asked.

She was looking forward to what Aris would pick now that she had sampled all the flavors.

"The crème chantilly cake is the tastiest," Aris replied. The cheesecake and the chocolate cake had both been delicious, but they couldn't compare to the delicate sweetness of the crème chantilly. "No wonder it's the most popular flavor."

There were plenty of other cakes available, but the crème chantilly always seemed to run out faster. Everyone who had been to the café before knew to stock up on that cake while they could.

"Next time, I'll have to eat as much crème chantilly as I can." Aris took another sip of her drink, which had been made with freshly juiced strawberries and honey. It was sweet and delicious. "I guess there's a reason it's so expensive,"

The café was buffet-style, with an entrance fee paid upfront. High prices were justified by the luxurious ingredients—the cakes and drinks were made with expensive honey. The café's food was that of the highest quality in the empire.

"I'm glad I skipped breakfast today," Aris said, happy to be filling up on cake.

She got up with her plate to get more crème chantilly, Violet following close behind her. The girls both placed more slices of crème chantilly on their plates. Aris smiled as she looked down at her plate, which was completely full again. Little strawberries had been placed delicately on top of the cakes. If only she could eat like this every day.

"My lady."

"Yes?"

"You'll have to watch what you eat again starting tomorrow," Lucine said, clicking her tongue disapprovingly at how much food Aris had brought back. She was eating far more than she usually did.

"I ate that much?"

"Yes," Lucine nodded gravely.

"Lady Violet," Anthe spoke up.

"Hmm?"

"This applies to you too."

Both maids were thinking the same thing. They would let their young ladies eat as they pleased today, but tomorrow was a whole 'nother story.

"I thought I wouldn't have to diet anymore," Aris sighed.

It looked like she'd only be eating salads for the foreseeable future.

"Me too," Violet agreed, echoing her sigh.

Eating delicious food made the girls happy, but it would surely fatten them up. It was a tragedy.

"Are you going to diet with me, Lucine?" Aris asked, looking pointedly at Lucine's plate. It didn't look much different from hers.

"Ah."

"You're going to diet with me, right?"

If Aris had to suffer, she wasn't going to do it alone. She stared Lucine down almost threateningly.

"Yes," Lucine replied, eventually giving in.

"I hate dieting."

"Me too." Aris and Violet commiserated.

They couldn't help but yearn over the thought of dieting.

Lucine looked at their pitiful faces, and eventually with a sigh, said, "Very well. You can eat whatever you want once a week."

To appease her lady, Lucine was offering Aris the choice of eating something she liked once a week. An the nodded in agreement—it was only natural to have stronger cravings when dieting, and to avoid binge-eating. The smarter choice would be to allow their ladies to eat well once a week.

"I'm going to eat as much as I can today," Aris decided, looking at her cake with determination.

No matter how much cake she ate, she never tired of it. If only she would never gain weight! Taking another bite of cake, Aris smiled with glee.

"Big Sister… did you know that the Great Hunt will begin soon?"

"Yes? Ah." Aris nodded. Her father had always taken part in the hunt around this time of year. Aris had never been invited, so she had always stayed home. However, now that she had debuted, and was the most talked-about woman in the capital, it was likely that the emperor would demand her attendance, even if her father protested. "I wonder if I'll attend this year. I suspect I might be a Flower of the Hunt."

"I'll be participating in the hunt," Violet said.

"Participating?" Aris was surprised at Violet's words.

Violet didn't look the type to be skilled with weapons.

"Yes, I'll be hunting this year. I'm a decent archer."

"My goodness!" Aris pictured Violet, wearing pants and riding on horseback. "Just thinking about it is impressive."

"Thank you," Violet said with a grin. "I ought to know how to fight if I'm ever to become the duchess, so I've been learning little by little."

Aris studied Violet with fascination. She was exceptionally wise and talented for her age. "Since you're competing, you should aim for first place!"

"I don't think that will be possible, but I'll at least try to shoot a small fowl."

"Say, Violet, after we finish eating, would you please accompany me to purchase some sealing wax?" Aris asked, changing the subject.

"Sealing wax? For your letters?" Violet asked.

"Yes."

Aris had thought her envelopes had looked a little plain, so she decided on adding a wax seal. She hoped Roy would appreciate the design left on the little pool of wax.

"You put so much effort into these letters! The least he could do is respond," Violet pouted.

Aris laughed softly and shook her head. "I don't expect anything in return when I send the letters. That's asking a lot from the other person."

Roy had a reserved, serious personality. If she wanted to approach him, she had to do so slowly and with care. If the situation was reversed, that would be the only way she would feel comfortable receiving the letters.

Once the girls had finished their cakes, they headed out to purchase sealing wax and stamps. As they sat in the carriage, Aris mulled over what design she should buy.

"What about a stamp with a moon design?" Violet suggested. "I think the moon suits you, Big Sister."

"A moon?" Aris was puzzled. After all, she didn't possess pale golden hair that shimmered like moonlight, or anything like that.

"It's gentle and calm, just like you," Violet continued.

Aris considered it for a moment before breaking into a smile. "I'll do that, then."

The moon felt a little more special, now that Violet said it suited her. Then the carriage came to a stop, and the girls entered the stationery shop. The store was bustling and full of customers.

"Welcome," a sales clerk greeted Violet and Aris as they walked in. It was apparent they were wealthy nobles, as they were accompanied by their maids. The clerk tilted his head as he observed Aris. He couldn't quite place where he had seen her before. "Are you ladies looking for anything in particular?"

"I'm looking for a wax stamp with a moon design."

The clerk led them to a nearby counter. There, Aris could see several stamps decorated with moons. The stamps were displayed neatly, with little cards placed next to each stamp, showcasing the impression left when pressed into wax. She could choose her favorite design from the cards before her.

Aris examined each stamp, but one particular design soon caught her eye. It was of a large crescent moon, with a smaller crescent moon nestled inside. To her, the two moons seemed to resemble a couple in a loving embrace. She was pleased by the design. The bigger moon represented her, she decided, while the smaller moon was Roy.

"I'll take this one."

"Are you done selecting?" Violet asked.

"Yes."

"I'll look for one for myself too."

Since she was there, Violet also decided to purchase a stamp, as they were quite useful in everyday life. Magic existed in this world, but only in rare quantities. Letters were still the primary form of communication, so stationary was a necessity. Wax stamps and seals were popular items to decorate letters and envelopes.

"I already have a few sealing stamps at home," Violet said, as she selected a stamp with five stars etched into it. "Though I'm always open to adding to my collection."

Nodding in agreement, Aris also continued to peruse the rest of the store's stamp selection to see if there was another design she liked. However, nothing appealed to her as much as her moon stamp. Soon the girls placed their stamps inside their shopping basket and headed to the register.

"Is this your first time at our store?" the owner of the store asked.

Aris nodded her head. "It is."

"We issue a monthly catalog of new stamp designs. Would you be interested in subscribing?"

He did say that new designs were released each month. What girl could resist the temptation to look at pretty things?

Aris felt compelled to nod again. "Yes, I'd like that."

The shopkeeper pushed the contact form towards her. "Write your address here, please."

Aris smiled and wrote her home address, as did Violet. As they did so, the owner's eyes grew wide. He'd thought that the brunette certainly looked familiar, but he now quickly realized she was Lady Aris, the young lady whose picture was in all the newspapers.

"It's an honor to meet you, my lady," he said, bowing his head.

Nobles would occasionally visit his store, but influential figures such as Lady Aris usually sent their maids instead.

Aris and Violet exited the shop after paying for their stamps.

"I hope we get to see a lot of pretty designs," Violet said, already excited to receive the catalog. She looked forward to expanding her collection with as many pretty stamps as she could get.

"Me too," Aris concurred.

Violet escorted Aris back home in her carriage, and the girls exchanged promises to meet again soon. Aris headed up to her bedroom. When she had settled in, she took out her newly purchased stamp and pressed it into some melted wax. She lifted the stamp to reveal two perfect crescent moons.

"How pretty."

"Why didn't you get more designs?" Lucine asked, noticing how pleased Aris looked.

The stamp that Aris had been using before had been the Horissen family crest. It was exciting to finally use a different design.

"I didn't really like anything else."

"Really?"

"Yes," Aris said, clearing a space on her desk to store her stamp. The handle gleamed in the light. "I want to write another letter soon."

However, it had not been long since her last letter to Roy. If she wrote him too often, she might scare him away. After all, the purpose of her letters was to create a friendship with Roy.

"Then write a letter to Lady Violet. Do you have to write letters to that man only?"

"Huh?" Aris hadn't thought of that. Lucine had a point; it was perfectly acceptable to write letters to Violet as well. Lucine could tell that Aris was itching to use her new stamp. "You're a genius, Lucine!"

"Am I?" Lucine asked, shrugging her shoulders. "I just want the best for you."

"Then how about you don't make me diet?"

"That I can't do!" Lucine had trimmed Aris' hair and was now deftly applying hair oils along its lengths. It was the secret behind Aris' gorgeous locks. "You should get some rest now."

"Yes."

It was already time to sleep. Aris climbed into bed, and Lucine extinguished the lamp before exiting the room. As Aris closed her eyes, her thoughts drifted to Roy.

I should tell him about the cake café.

Her letters always comprised the events of her daily life. They were the stories one would typically send to close friends, but she hoped her future husband liked them, too.

Hmm.

If she kept sending him letters, surely, he'd respond at some point.

She remained optimistic.

The lights in the elegant bar glowed brightly. Beneath them stood a large group of noblemen. Many aristocrats frequented the bar, so the owner always kept a few large rooms unoccupied in case they dropped by. However, he hadn't been expecting such a large group of nobles, and immediately felt nervous. He could not afford to make any mistakes tonight.

The owner quickly led the group of noblemen to one of the empty rooms and turned the lamp on. The light flickered in the round lampshade, and as the men settled into their seats, the owner began taking their orders.

"I want something strong."

"Any preference, sir?"

"Whatever is fine," Ian replied.

The owner bowed his head. "Understood. It might be a little intense."

"Good."

Ian intended to get drunk tonight. First, there had been the situation with the Crown Prince's birthday, and now this happened. He was a disappointment to his daughter. He wanted to drown his sadness with alcohol.

"Don't drink too much at once. You'll get drunk too soon," Louison said. He was in unusually high spirits. Everyone around him eyed him in jealousy, and with good reason; his daughter would participate in this year's Great Hunt, but not as a Flower of the Hunt. "You're supposed to savor the alcohol, not chug it down."

"You don't know how I feel, Duke," Ian groaned disconsolately.

Soon thereafter, the owner of the bar returned with the drinks. Ian was not the only member of the party to order a potent drink. Many other nobles in attendance also had daughters that had been selected as Flowers of the Hunt. Indeed, all the men who felt they had failed as fathers had gathered to have a drink. Ian poured the alcohol into glasses and passed them out amongst the men.

"A toast, in the hopes that our daughters will not be chosen!"

"Cheers!"

The men clinked their glasses together, muttering silent prayers that their daughters would not become the Lady of the Hunt. One drink turned into two, followed swiftly by a third, then fourth, fifth, and so on.

Ian, tipsy, cocked his head. The owner had warned him that the liquor would be strong, and he hadn't lied. Ian already felt a little drunk.

"How long has she been learning to hunt?" Ian asked Louison, as he struggled to prop his body upright.

Louison was still sober, and therefore able to give Ian an answer. "Since she was quite young."

"Since she was young?"

"My daughter has always been ambitious. That's why I let her do whatever she wants."

"Why didn't I make Aris learn how to hunt and use weapons?" Ian asked, his voice full of regret. "I need another drink."

He reached for the bottle again, but Louison gently blocked his hand.

"That's enough. Stop drinking." Louison patted Ian's shoulder. "You're drunk. Your daughter might not even be chosen."

However, Ian was full of doubts. "You know how famous my daughter is right now. How could she not be chosen? The chances are slim to none."

At that moment, one man spoke up, "It's more than likely that Lady Horissen will be picked."

Everyone sipped their drinks and looked at Ian. They all secretly hoped that his daughter would be chosen as the Lady of the Hunt. That was the only way that their own daughters would be safe.

"It would be best if you didn't say things like that," Louison said, silencing the man who had spoken.

Ian felt troubled—he was upset that everyone thought this way about his daughter.

Suddenly, one noble began singing a song about how his daughter was too young. Another man joined in. Louison, watching the men's drunken behavior, sighed. He knew all too well that if Violet had been a Flower instead of a huntress, he would have been doing the same.

"Ian!"

Louison tried to stop the man from drinking any more alcohol, but it was of no use.

Ian had to drink to drown his guilt.

Aris had woken up early that morning. She changed into her daytime attire and headed down to the lower floor. At the dining table, she saw Ian clearly nursing a massive headache. He looked terrible. A bowl of soup sat in front of him, but he had barely touched it.

"Father, are you okay?"

"Aris," Ian said, lifting his head as she walked in. "I just had a little too much to drink last night."

Even dressed casually, his daughter was objectively beautiful. Part of her popularity was because of the crown prince, but even without him, she would have caught the eyes of everyone around her, eventually. She resembled her mother. Ian felt his heart break.

Aris sat down across from her father and began eating the soup and bread placed before her. She observed her father, who was clearly still lacking an appetite, as he sat with his bread untouched.

"Why did you drink last night?"

Aris had rarely seen her father drink. If she thought about it, it was rare the two would have breakfast together too—usually, Ian would rise and have breakfast early, before retiring to his study or setting off for the palace long before Aris awoke.

"I was just a little upset," Ian said with a sigh. He didn't have the heart to break it to her. He'd failed to protect her again but knew that he couldn't put it off. "Actually, I have something to tell you. It seems that you'll be attending the hunt as a Flower."

"I will? Ah... alright then," she replied nonchalantly as she continued with her meal.

Ian glanced at Aris—to his surprise. She didn't seem bothered by the news. "Are you alright with that?"

"It sounds like a hassle, but it is my duty," Aris said with a small shrug. It wasn't something she could decline just because she wished to; if she didn't have the power to change the outcome, why not conserve the energy rather than waste it fighting unwinnable battles. "Since I was the crown prince's partner at the ball, I suppose I'll need to make an effort to dress nicely for the occasion."

Naturally, Lucine would handle all the details of her outfit.

Ah!

Aris realized this also meant she'd be required to go on an even stricter diet, a prospect she dreaded.

Aris glanced at him, who still wore a look of defeat. "You don't want me to go, do you, Father?"

He nodded in response.

"But there's nothing we can do about it. Honestly, I'm not terribly pleased about this either," Aris said, looking at him in the eye. "But I understand that I have no choice in the matter."

The emperor had already expressed his interest in her as a potential crown princess—it was natural that he would request her attendance. If Aris had been in his position, she too would have wanted the crown prince's first dance partner to be present. Aris kept a cool head and thought about the situation pragmatically. There was nothing more foolish than keeping one's hopes up about something unchangeable. Even if Aris protested, the outcome would be no different.

"I should inform Lucine."

"I'm sorry," Ian said apologetically.

"Don't be," Aris said reassuringly.

After all, who would dare oppose the emperor's command?

"Ah, so that's why you drank!" Aris grumbled, putting the pieces together.

A slight flush colored his cheeks. He was already in his forties, and was at the point in life where he needed to take better care of his health.

Aris smiled and expressed her concern for her father's wellbeing. "Don't drink so much next time. You should take care of yourself."

"I won't."

It was such a shame that he would have to marry off his angelic daughter someday.

Kkamang Kkamang

"You're attending the Great Hunt? I wonder what dress you should wear," Lucine mused, already expressing concern.

Despite having ordered several new dresses to prepare for the crown prince's ball, Lucine continued to worry whether Aris had a sufficient wardrobe.

"Yes, well, I don't think we need to call in another dressmaker," Aris replied.

"I agree." Lucine nodded.

Aris' wardrobe was filled with the season's latest styles from the capital's leading dressmaker. She planned to choose from one of those dresses for the hunt.

"I won't have to dress up as much as last time, will I?" Aris asked.

The Great Hunt wasn't as significant an event as the crown prince's ball, so she expected she wouldn't need to spend as much time preparing. At least, that was what she thought.

"What are you talking about? You need to look spectacular," Lucine said, her eyes twinkling. "You are the face of the empire."

"Lucine. I'm really not!" Aris protested.

"You're the lady that the crown prince chose for his first dance," Lucine said firmly.

It was then that Aris acutely understood Hiel's reasoning for selecting her as his first dance partner. Even Lucine was making a big fuss; she couldn't imagine how the other ladies would have felt if they'd been chosen.

"We'll need to weigh you."

"What?" Aris yelped.

She had eaten large amounts of cake yesterday, so it was likely she'd gained some weight.

I don't want to weigh myself.

However, the nagging continued until Aris stepped on the scale, which only earned her a sharp look from Lucine, who promptly declared, "Today's lunch will be salad."

"Alright," Aris said, crestfallen.

It wasn't that Aris disliked vegetables, she simply didn't appreciate having to eat them for the sake of dieting.

"Once you're back to your original weight, I'll let you have something delicious," Lucine coaxed gently.

Aris lit up with excitement. "Really? Alright then."

"Lady Violet will probably diet too," Lucine said, trying to soothe Aris.

"Violet is attending as a huntress, not a Flower," Aris said, frowning. She probably wouldn't need to diet at all. "Besides, it doesn't make me feel any better thinking that Violet isn't eating either."

She could never get used to these diets.

It was a sunny day, with nary a cloud to be seen in the clear blue sky. Aris had awoken early to be primped and plucked at the hands of Lucine. After being clothed in a suitable dress and having her makeup done, she looked as beautiful as ever. Aris appraised herself with critical eyes—she didn't possess Violet's stunning looks, but she would probably outshine the other ladies.

"It must be nice to be you, my lady," Lucine gazed admiringly. "You're beautiful—

"What? Ah yes." Aris was confused for a moment — in her previous world, she'd been rather plain, but in this world, she was a beauty. "Though it can be a real pain sometimes."

"Is that so?" Lucine said.

Aris nodded in response.

There were plenty of unwanted inconveniences that came with beauty. The novel had started right before the two main characters had married, but she had entered the story far earlier than those events would occur. Over the years, she'd experienced much more than she'd ever imagined.

"Today's hunt is a headache too."

Even though she was attending as a Flower, she only intended to chat with the other ladies and then return home. It was a shame Violet wouldn't be there with her.

"I guess you have a point," Lucine said. "My lady, should I bring a book for you?"

"Ah! That would be nice," Aris said, as she eagerly nodded her head.

If there were no interesting ladies to converse with, Aris might be forced to sit by herself. She hadn't considered that possibility, but Lucine had been clever enough to ask. Reading a book was another good way to pass the time. She watched happily as Lucine packed a book into her bags.

Ian took Aris' hand as she descended the staircase. He couldn't help but marvel at how his daughter's beauty grew by the day. She would surely attract the attention of every man at the hunt. Not only was her appearance gorgeous, but she also had a kind personality. Men would be unable to resist her.

"A carriage from the palace is waiting for us," Ian said. "I heard it was sent by the crown prince."

Aris nodded. The crown prince had said that he wanted to be friends, and he was true to his word. He had sent her a carriage when he learned she would attend the hunt. The palace carriage was ornate, with the royal coat of arms adorning the sides. Aris was impressed at the plushness of the cushions. The marquis' carriage, although grand, was nowhere near as luxurious as the palace's carriages.

"It feels wonderful," Aris said, stroking the soft fabric of the cushions.

"Indeed," Ian replied, as he seated himself across from her.

Seeing the two seated, the footman shut the door.

Lucine would travel in a separate carriage, and Aris was excited to spend some time alone with her father.

"Who will be participating in the hunt today?" Aris asked, eager to find out.

"Well, the crown prince will be there," Ian replied.

"Of course," Aris said, nodding. Apparently, it was a big deal that he would participate in the hunt. "Is he good with weapons?"

"I've heard that he can hold his own," Ian responded.

"I see. Who else?" Aris asked.

"Hmm." Ian racked his brains thinking about the contestant list. "I heard some warriors will be in attendance."

"Oh my. Well, the hunt is a good place to make a name for yourself," Aris said.

The crown prince could never beat skilled warriors in a duel, no matter how hard he tried. However, a hunt was a different matter. There was no telling who would win. So why would the warriors attend? If they outshone the crown prince, he would surely hold a grudge against them. It would almost be better for them not to hunt to the best of their abilities.

"Did the crown prince hunt last year?"

"No," Ian said, "the crown prince didn't participate last year. Now that he has become of age, this will be the first official hunt that he has been allowed to participate in."

"Ah."

Well then, there was nothing left to say; the winner was already predetermined. Who would dare outshine the crown prince at his first hunt? Aris let out a beleaguered sigh. At this rate, she would have to dance with him again. She couldn't stop her thoughts from running wild.

"I should ask the crown prince to dance with someone else today," Aris said coolly.

Ian nodded in agreement.

He had been thinking the same thing.

Hiel was gazing in the mirror again. His long blond hair had been pulled into a short ponytail, and he was outfitted in hunting gear and a hat with a feather pinned to the side.

"Absolutely dashing," he remarked to himself, as he marveled at his reflection.

"You're quite right, Your Royal Majesty," Razaen chimed in zealously. He launched into a long speech, lavishing Hiel with praises, as he was often won't to do.

Hiel felt his self-esteem rising with each passing second. He certainly enjoyed receiving compliments. However, it was the people who didn't compliment him he kept as his friends, as it often meant that they had no ulterior motives.

"The carriages must have arrived at Lady Essel and Lady Horissen's estates, right?" Hiel asked.

"Of course, Your Royal Highness."

Razaen was skilled at flattery, but he was even better at his job. Hiel loved having someone around who would sing his praises, but he had no use for a gentleman-in-waiting who couldn't do his job correctly. That was why all of his direct servants were not only skilled flatterers but also excellent workers.

Razaen looked at Hiel, his eyes sparkling expectantly. He was the one who had suggested that Hiel send carriages to the two ladies. Palace carriages were special. Once it became known that the ladies had arrived in palace carriages, everyone would know that Hiel held them in high regard.

"It was a splendid idea," Hiel acknowledged. Marquis Horissen and Duke Essel were both avid supporters of the crown. It couldn't hurt to be friendly with them and their families. "You'll receive a bonus this month."

"Thank you, Your Royal Highness," Razaen said, with a bow.

"I demand to see the crown prince!" A woman's voice screeched.

There was a great deal of commotion coming from outside. The crown prince turned his head and peered out the door. It seemed like someone was causing a scene in front of his room.

"Should we have her removed?" Razaen asked indifferently.

It was obviously one of the crown prince's mistresses who had mistaken his attention to mean anything more than a simple dalliance.

Hiel laughed. "No, let her in."

At his command, Razaen opened the doors. An alluring young woman bolted into the room, clearly distraught.

"What seems to be the matter?"

The woman began sobbing, her tears as large as pearls. "Your Royal Highness, why aren't you taking me to the hunt?"

She had fully expected the crown prince to bring her to the Great Hunt with him.

"Why should I bring you along?" Hiel asked, as he peered at her curiously. He approached her and patted her shoulder. "That's the type of event I would only bring my lover to."

"Your Royal Highness!" she protested.

"If you consider your time with me special, I advise you to stop now," he warned. "You're not my lover, you're a mistress."

"Your Royal Highness," she whined again.

"I told you never to forget that, last night."

Just last night, the crown prince had treated her with tenderness and care. They had spent a passionate night together, and the woman had fully believed that he would take her to the hunt the next day.

"It's really difficult for me when you act like this," he sighed, running a hand through his hair. "You should head back now."

"Your Royal Highness!" she wailed, realizing her tears failed to move him.

The crown prince enjoyed being praised and indulging in good fun, but he always maintained clear boundaries. He breezed past his crying mistress and walked out the door. No matter where he went, he would always be the center of attention, and women would always desire him. He liked that. However, he wouldn't stand for any woman who tried to cross the line.

"What a pain," Hiel remarked. "It's not easy being this popular."

"Indeed," Razaen said.

In actuality, it wasn't just women who endeavored to attach themselves to him; men would also approach him, intending to gain his favor. Hiel found it amusing, but he always kept them at arm's length. Occasionally, he would encounter those that actually preferred to maintain a distance and showed no interest in cultivating a closer relationship. These were the people that he wanted to befriend—they wouldn't expect any favorable treatment, and would always be honest with him. Such people were few and far between, but by some stroke of luck, he had discovered two such individuals!

I haven't seen them in a while.

He looked forward to seeing his friends again at the hunt.

Even with a magically enchanted carriage, it still took nearly two hours to arrive at the hunting grounds. The grounds were the personal property of the royal family, and lush foliage could be seen spread out for acres. A building had been constructed specifically for the Great Hunt thirty minutes from the forest entrance. To avoid congestion from the sudden arrival of a bevy of carriages, only ladies selected as Flowers of the Hunt could arrive via carriage; the gentlemen were required to arrive on horseback. An overabundance of carriages would surely result in a traffic jam.

A separate passage was reserved for use by palace carriages. Aris encountered limited traffic and was set to arrive earlier than all the other ladies. As she gazed out her window, she soon noticed another carriage bearing the royal coat of arms. It didn't appear to belong to the crown prince, but seemed to be another escort carriage sent as a present from Hiel.

Could that be Violet?

She had an inkling that it might be. The carriage came to a halt, and Aris and Ian alighted together. The other carriage pulled up next to them and let its passengers out.

"Violet!" Aris squealed with excitement.

Violet had stepped out of the carriage, dressed in pants.

I knew it.

"Big Sister," Violet called out, waving as soon as she recognized her.

Louison, who had been in the carriage with Violet, spotted Ian from afar. Ian nodded to the duke.

"The crown prince sent us a carriage," Louis remarked, as he strolled up to Ian.

"Likewise," Ian replied.

"I'd originally planned on riding my horse here," Louison said, as he watched the two girls chattering away.

Violet was attending as a huntress, and Aris as a flower.

"I heard this is the crown prince's first hunt," Aris remarked.

Violet nodded, immediately catching the implication.

"The hunt will surely boost his public image," she replied.

Aris sighed, asking dejectedly, "He won't try to dance with me again, will he?".

Violet gave her an uncertain look. "You might be chosen by the winner, Big Sister."

The crown prince loathed things he considered bothersome. Therefore, it was highly likely he would select a flower that would be the least troublesome. Aris fit the bill.

"Don't say that," Aris grumbled.

"Well, alright," Violet said, grinning innocently. When she smiled, it seemed like everything around her brightened.

"Your smile has improved a lot," Aris noted.

"I've been practicing, just as you instructed."

Aris had an extremely beautiful smile, and Violet had always envied it. The older girl had taught her how she practiced smiling. In her previous life, she had worked as a salesperson at a supermarket. She was regularly trained on how to leave customers with an amiable impression, and part of her training was to smile in a welcoming and warm manner. Even after awakening as

Aris, she continued to practice her smile. Violet was a quick learner. With a little guidance from Aris, she had instantly picked up on all of Aris' tips and her smile had become brighter and more natural.

"I wanted you to be the first person to see my smile."

She certainly had a way with words. Violet flashed another smile, and Aris found she couldn't help but reciprocate.

"If I was a man, I'm sure I would have already married you," Aris said with a laugh.

"Really?" Violet said cheerfully.

"Absolutely." Aris grinned.

"I suppose that would work out since you wouldn't want to be more powerful than me, Big Sister."

Aris wasn't one to dream of power and glory. She had always stated that her dream was to live a simple, comfortable life.

Suddenly, a carriage barreled in before coming to an abrupt stop in front of the girls. It was ornately decorated, and so ostentatious it could be spotted from a mile away. It reminded the girls of a certain someone. As if on cue, Hiel flung open the door and hopped out of the carriage, flipping his long blond hair.

"Ah," he said, as he spotted Aris and Violet.

"Good day, Your Royal Highness," Ian and Louison said, bowing.

Violet and Aris greeted him as well.

"It's been a while," Hiel replied amiably. Noticing Violet was dressed in pants, he turned to her and said genuinely, "I heard you'll be taking part in the hunt. I hope you'll be a good opponent,"

"Yes, Your Royal Highness," Violet replied, realizing he truly meant it. "I'm honored to be here."

"Aris, you look beautiful as always," Hiel said, turning to address her.

"Thank you," Aris replied, looking at Hiel. She started the day with a compliment. "You look dashing today as well."

"Do I? Well, of course I do," Hiel said, accepting her praise and looking obviously pleased. He was as arrogant as ever. "Oh, right… If I win, I'll be dancing with you."

Aris' jaw dropped at Hiel's statement. Her worst fears had been realized. It took her a moment to regain her wits, but she promptly responded in a flat tone, "I'm not emotionally prepared for this honor. Please choose someone else to dance with!"

Hiel grinned, as though she'd told a funny joke. "I was hoping you would react like that."

"Your Royal Highness!" Aris cried out in exasperation.

"Nothing annoying will happen to me if I dance with you." Hiel chuckled.

This jerk!

There was a reason he had wanted to be friends with her! She was the perfect foil to avoid potentially sticky situations. Aris, realizing this, huffed with irritation. At this rate, she'd really be irrevocably tied to Hiel.

"You're not really that dashing," Aris said, desperately holding back the rage bubbling inside. "In fact, you're not charming at all."

Hiel looked at her incredulously. "What? Why not?"

"Nothing is charming or dashing about a man who ignores a lady's request!" Aris said snippily before storming off towards Ian.

Appalled at being told he was neither charming nor dashing, Hiel remained frozen in shock.

"I dare you to say that again!" He bellowed.

Hiel glared at Razaen, who wished he could seal Aris' mouth to keep her from speaking any further.

Aris quickly ducked behind Ian.

"I'm telling you this because we're friends, but you don't look good in black. Your outfit at the ball was much better!" She blurted out whatever crossed her mind. Even though she'd exacted a small piece of revenge, it wasn't nearly enough to quell her frustrations.

I'll see you at the ball!

She'd stomp all over his feet again!

All the participants of the hunt had gathered in the Great Hall. Inside the new building, the Flowers had broken off into smaller groups. The men congregated together while the ladies sat and chatted with each other. All the hunters were having conversations on horseback as they waited for the hunt to begin.

"I'll be over there." Violet mounted her horse with practiced ease.

Aris thought her quite impressive. She held her hands together and looked up at the younger girl.

"Do well out there," Aris said, wishing the young girl a stroke of good luck.

"I'll just be catching some small game," Violet replied with a smile.

She turned her horse and headed towards the group of hunters. Her blonde ponytail swung in time with each trot.

Louison followed close behind, and the two soon rode side by side on their horses.

"Father, you should go too," Aris said, turning to Ian.

"Alright," Ian responded with a nod.

Most nobles attended the Great Hunt out of a sense of duty and propriety, so Ian would also be participating as a hunter. Aris waved goodbye to her father as he rode off on his horse.

"We should head inside," Lucine said, pointing to the hall.

"Violet won't be there," Aris remarked glumly.

"Are you already bored? What if you tried to befriend another young lady?" Lucine asked, trying to cheer Aris up.

"Another lady?" Aris pondered the suggestion.

She had received several social invitations, especially since the crown prince's ball, but Aris had not been particularly inclined to accept any of them. The daughters of countless counts and dukes had reached out to her, and there seemed to be a great interest in making her acquaintance.

"Even if you hadn't danced with the crown prince, you still would have received invitations," Lucine said.

Certainly, Aris' popularity had risen after her dance with the crown prince, but she would've attracted attention, regardless. Not only was she the only daughter of the Horissen family, but she was also rumored to be kind, smart, and beautiful.

"Really?" Aris asked.

"Absolutely," Lucine said.

Aris mulled over Lucine's words as they entered the hall. As soon as she entered, people's attention would be focused on her.

What do I even say? Aris fretted.

She'd received attention in the past, but she was always accompanied by Violet, so the attention had been shared between the two. She'd also never had to engage in conversation with several people before, but this time would be different. Violet was gone, and she was by herself.

As expected, as she entered the hall everyone's gazes turned towards her. Aris pretended not to mind, and smiled genially, making eye contact with those around her. She soon found her assigned seat, which bore the inscription of *Lady Aris Horissen* on the back of her chair, and promptly seated herself.

"I'll be over there." Once Lucine had ensured Aris was settled in, she headed to the back of the hall where all the maids had congregated.

Aris sighed as Lucine, too, left her.

"Good day," the young lady next to her said, striking up a conversation.

Aris turned towards her and flashed a brilliant smile that lit up her face and evoked a kind, angelic impression.

The smile was so effective, it left the young lady briefly dazzled. Regaining her composure, she said, "My name is Azelle Lawson."

"Are you perhaps Count Lawson's daughter?" Aris asked.

Aris recalled Count Lawson to be on good terms with her father, and she recognized the young lady from the crown prince's tea party. Azelle was a lovely young woman with flowing blue hair and sky-blue eyes.

"Yes, that's me," Azelle replied. "I haven't seen you since the tea party; I had no idea we'd be seated next to each other."

Azelle proved to be an easy conversation partner — as they had met before, the conversation flowed smoothly. Aris noted Azelle was dressed in an elaborate, eye-catching gown.

"I love your dress," she said.

Azelle let out a deep sigh. Making a pained face, she said, "My maid picked it out for me, although truthfully, I don't like standing out."

"Oh, why not? You might catch a nice gentleman's eye if you stand out," Aris said.

At this, Azelle quickly shook her head, as if that would be a terrible thing. "My father wouldn't want that to happen,"

Somehow, that reasoning sounded familiar to Aris. She'd heard that many members of the royal court were very protective of their daughters, and guessed Count Lawson was one of them.

Aris lowered her voice to a whisper and asked in a hushed tone. " Did he try and fail to keep you from attending the tea party, too?"

"That's right. The day he failed to prevent me from being selected as a Flower, he came home drunk," Azelle groused, sighing as she recalled the events of that day.

Aris laughed. "My father did the same."

"Marquis Horissen did?" Azelle giggled.

Aris thought Azelle was a striking young lady, but the crown prince had shown no interest simply because she was not blonde. In fact, the seating arrangements for the hunt had been determined according to the crown prince's preference rather than by title. The front row was filled with the blonde ladies the crown prince had shown favor to at the tea party.

"I've always considered it odd, though," Azelle said, before pausing. "Lady Horissen... you didn't speak to the crown prince much that day, yet you were selected as his dance partner."

"Hmm? Well, yes, that's true," Aris agreed.

"And you're not seated in the front row, you're sitting next to me," Azelle continued.

It wasn't just Azelle—the other ladies had also realized the peculiarity of the situation, and had whispered amongst each other.

"Well, I suppose there's a difference between the people the crown prince favors, and the people he is really close to," Azelle said, trying to wrap her head around Hiel's strange behavior.

There sure is.

After all, he had only chosen her out of convenience. *I didn't want to sit in the front row anyway.*

Aris turned her attention outside. The emperor had wrapped up his opening remarks, and Aris could see Violet heading towards the hunting grounds. As Violet rode her horse expertly, she seemed to shine brighter than anyone else in the world. Aris watched as Hiel steered his horse steadily and pulled up next to Violet. He turned to address her, as well as Louison and Ian, but she struggled to make out what was being said.

"I can never tell what the crown prince is thinking," Aris remarked, to which Azelle nodded in agreement.

The two ladies continued to pass the time in merry conversation, covering a wide range of topics from the tea party to their daily lessons, and even the latest trends in dresses.

Lucine, who had been keeping watch from a distance, was relieved that her lady had found herself an amiable companion—even though Aris could easily fit in anywhere, Lucine couldn't help but be a worrywart.

"You're Lady Horissen's maid?"

The group of maids that had been discussing the ladies they served all reacted in surprise to Lucine's introduction.

Lucine was slightly taken aback by their response and peered down at her outfit. She wasn't dressed too plainly... was she? Her outfit was modestly befitting of her status, but she had applied light makeup in honor of the occasion.

"Ah, am I underdressed?" Lucine asked.

"No! No, it's not that! We were just envious that you work at the Horissen estate," one maid quickly clarified.

Everyone nodded their heads in agreement.

The master of the estate, Ian, was widely known to be a kind and good-natured master—the Horissen estate was considered an excellent place to work, and those that did, chose to remain there until retirement. Lucine, who thought about Aris and her soft temperament, couldn't help but agree.

"My lady always listens to what I have to say," Lucine remarked.

"She even listens to your opinions?"

"When I recommend a dress to my lady, she always says it's not to her liking and insists I bring out another."

"My lady has the worst mood swings."

The other maids piped up one after another, commiserating about the struggles and woes they faced serving their young ladies. Listening to them chat, Lucine was once again reminded what a wonderful person her lady was—she was proud that Aris considered her as a friend and not just one of her helpers.

"If you don't mind my asking, please share who the seamstress was for Lady Horissen's dress?" One girl asked with curiosity.

The request was echoed by the others, and the girls all turned to look at Lucine, waiting with bated breath.

Lucine straightened her posture and tucked a strand of hair behind her ear. She could feel her confidence rising as she realized she had their rapt attention—this was her moment to shine.

"My lady looks good in everything, so it doesn't really matter what she wears," she began smugly, "but, of course, I can't allow her to be seen in just any old dress. She is a Horissen, after all."

"Of course," another voice concurred.

Glancing at the speaker, Lucine could tell that she was a clever, quick-witted maid.

"So, what I do is..." Lucine began divulging her tricks of the trade to her captivated audience, who eagerly committed her every word to memory.

If they informed their ladies that their dresses were from the same boutique frequented by Lady Aris Horissen, there would be no complaints ever again.

"What do you think about traveling together?" Hiel asked.

Violet considered the crown prince's offer carefully. If she followed him, then so would her father. They were all fellow competitors in the hunt, but the crown prince would be entitled to the first claim of ownership over any game spotted.

As if aware of her concerns, Hiel said, "You said you just wanted to catch a little small game. I know a spot with a lot of game. I can guide you there, and then we can split up and head our separate ways."

"Yes, thank you," Violet agreed. It was hard to decline when he offered like that.

"It's nothing." Hiel nodded, and the two began riding into the woods, with Louison following a few paces behind. They had made it nearly halfway up a mountain when Hiel slowed to a stop. "This is the spot with the most game."

It was time for them to part ways. The crown prince left, guiding his horse towards the location he'd previously mapped out. Violet steered her horse in another direction, with her father ever at her heels. Louison was a participant, but he had no intention of actually hunting. The only reason he had bothered to attend was to ensure his daughter's safety.

Soon Violet spotted a rabbit. She carefully took aim and released her arrow. The arrow shot forward and cleanly struck the small animal.

"I got it!" Violet cheered.

Louison dismounted and walked over to collect the rabbit and remove the arrow. "You have excellent aim."

"I'm not skilled with the sword, but I've always been an excellent shot." Arrows were more commonly used in hunting than swords. "It looks like it will be tasty."

As if on cue, her stomach growled at the thought of feasting on rabbit meat.

Louison smiled at his daughter.

"You'll have to receive permission from Anthe first," he teased.

After the girls had returned from their cake excursion, Anthe had placed Violet on a strict diet. Lucine had come to the hunt, but Anthe had not. Since Violet was attending as a huntress and not as a Flower, Louison had accompanied her instead.

"If I catch another, I'll gift it to Big Sister," Violet said.

After plucking out the arrow, Louison placed the dead rabbit into a sack. Each hunter was required to bring back their game in the sacks they had been provided.

"How many do you plan to hunt today?" he asked.

Violet held up three fingers. "Three."

"Isn't that too little?"

"It's just enough."

That would be enough for her to enjoy the day's hunt. Although it would be nice if she caught more, she didn't particularly want to. It didn't exactly bring her joy in killing living things. Yes, three would be just enough.

"There has to be something here," Hiel muttered to himself.

He had heard that wild boars frequented the area, and had decided to head over at the start of the hunt. If he captured a boar, he was guaranteed to be crowned the winner of the hunt. Catching a boar alone was no simple feat, but Hiel felt up to the challenge. It was his first hunt, and naturally, he wanted to win. He heard a rustling noise behind him, and he whirled around to find a wild boar sniffing the ground, still unaware of Hiel's presence. It was an enormous beast of a boar. If Hiel was successful, he'd be set. He smiled and prepared to take aim.

Suddenly, the boar took notice of Hiel, who had been nearly ready to shoot. The wild animal grunted loudly and quickly charged at him. He was in danger. Hiel thought back to his father's warning not to do anything dangerous without his guards. Just before the boar could reach him, an arrow zipped by and firmly lodged itself in the boar's head. Someone had shot an arrow at the last minute, killing the boar instantly.

"Are you alright?"

"Are you okay?"

Two familiar voices rang out from behind him. The crown prince let out a breath of relief before turning to look back. There, Violet and Louison stood, each holding their bows and arrows.

"How did you find me?" Hiel asked, still slightly dazed.

"We happened to be passing by when we spotted you," Violet said.

They thought they might be able to catch better prey if they headed in the same direction as the crown prince, but they had no idea they would end up saving his life.

"You mustn't go somewhere this dangerous without your guards," Louison said sternly. He needed to be stern, considering the crown prince's safety had been at risk.

"You're an excellent hunter," Hiel said to Violet.

It wasn't easy to catch a charging boar, but Violet had shot other arrow directly into the boar's skull.

Gesturing to the boar, he said, "Here, you caught this."

The crown prince easily relinquished ownership of the boar to Violet. Her eyes widened—she expected he would claim the beast for himself, but he was passing it over to her.

"I have a suggestion, Your Royal Highness," Violet said.

"What is it?" Hiel asked.

"Let's say that we caught it together," Violet continued, "you discovered it, and I shot it."

"But…" The crown prince was perplexed by Violet's words. Naturally, he wanted to be the star of the hunt, but he thought he'd missed his opportunity.

"You must be the star of this year's hunt," Violet said firmly.

"If I may, there are plenty of people who team up while hunting," Louison added. "It's not a bad idea."

"Are you sure?" The crown prince glanced at Violet's sack. "How many have you caught so far?"

"Three rabbits," Violet replied.

"And I've caught two quails," Louison added.

Hiel considered Violet's offer and agreed. Public interest in his performance was high this year. If he were to return now, he might even place last. He couldn't let that happen.

"Boars are heavy. I'm not sure this one will fit in our sacks," Violet said.

Violet was right.

The boar was too heavy for two grown men to carry, let alone a young lady.

"We should request assistance," Hiel said before lighting up his flare signal.

It was normally meant to be used by hunters as an emergency device if they ever found themselves in danger.

The flare soared into the sky.

"People will arrive soon."

"That's a relief." Violet smiled. Her smile was warm and charming, similar to Aris'.

"You smile like Aris now," Hiel remarked.

Violet's eyes twinkled. "I learned how to smile from Big Sister."

"A smart decision."

"I didn't learn for you, Your Royal Highness," she said firmly. She could never be too careful with him.

Hiel's mouth curled into a smile. "I know," he whispered to her.

Not long after, they spotted people running in their direction, responding to the emergency flare. A stretcher had also been brought in case there had been a medical injury, so it was quickly arranged to transport the boar back on the stretcher.

"Who will you dance with?"

Having caught a boar, it was almost guaranteed they would be named the joint winners of the hunt. Hiel was curious as to who Violet would choose as her dance partner.

"I don't know yet," Violet hummed, shrugging her shoulders. "Now I understand why you chose Big Sister Aris at the ball."

Violet didn't put much meaning in a dance at a place like this, but she worried that her partner would misconstrue their dance to be the start of something more.

"I'll let you in on a secret since you saved my life," Hiel said with a grin. "Dance with Limontri Raon."

"Yes, Your Royal Highness?" Violet asked, "Limontri Raon?"

"He's the younger son of Marquis Raon," Hiel said. "He's also my best friend."

"Ah." Violet said.

Best friends with the crown prince? Violet felt that she could guess what kind of person he was.

"He's the kind of fellow with no greed or ambition," Hiel continued.

"Much appreciated," Violet replied with a nod.

Indeed, this information was probably valuable enough to trade for saving his life. Now knowing who to select as her partner, Violet's expression brightened considerably.

The sky was showing the first wavering signs of sunset. Aris stood up from her seat and crossed the ballroom. The hunt had ended, and everyone had reconvened in the Great Hall. It was finally time to announce the winner and find out who had been selected as their dance partner. All the Flowers gathered at the front of the room.

The emperor surveyed the day's spoils before announcing the winner. "In first place, Crown Prince Hiel and Lady Violet!"

The crown prince and Violet had teamed up, as they had both been named the winners.

Aris sighed. Things were playing out exactly as she'd feared. The rules had stated that whoever caught a boar would be declared the winner, so why hadn't anyone else attempted to catch a boar? This was bad! Really bad! Meanwhile, Violet and Hiel had stepped onto the stage to receive their prize and congratulations from the emperor.

"I will announce the Flower I have selected now," the crown prince began, making eye contact with Aris from the stage. He had stared straight at her, ignoring the other ladies present. "Lady Aris Horissen."

As if it wasn't enough that he'd already chosen her for his first dance during the ball, he'd picked her yet again! She could feel everyone's stares prickling the back of her neck.

I'm not going to be the crown princess!

The crown prince had no intention of naming her as his betrothed, but others weren't privy to that knowledge.

Next, it was Violet's turn to name her Flower.

"I choose Limontri Raon," Violet announced.

Limontri Raon? The name sounded familiar. Aris recalled he was the younger son of Marquis Raon, but couldn't understand why Violet had chosen him.

The crowd's gazes turned towards someone in the crowd.

The young man looked annoyed as if he couldn't be bothered to deal with this. He certainly didn't look happy to have been chosen by Violet.

"You're so lucky!"

"She chose you!"

"Lady Essel called your name!"

All of his friends were buzzing with excitement, but the young man just sighed and said, "Don't make such a big deal out of it."

So that's what it was — the young man didn't read into any deeper meaning at having been selected and abhorred all the unnecessary attention and gossip it brought his way.

He was just like Aris.

"Aris Horissen, Limontri Raon," the emperor called out. "Please step forward."

Aris sighed and made her way to the front of the stage, as did Limontri.

Wow.

Violet was stunned by Limontri's good looks. He possessed long, pale silver hair and eyes that were a deep shade of crimson. He was so handsome that women couldn't help but stop in their tracks to stare in admiration.

"What do you think? He's alright, isn't he?" Hiel whispered.

"He's better looking than I had imagined," Violet answered honestly.

Meanwhile, Limontri was glaring at the crown prince. "Did you recommend me, Your Royal Highness?"

He had quickly deduced what had led Violet to choose him—it was at the crown prince's suggestion.

"Yup, it's always a pleasure to dance with a beautiful lady," Hiel said jovially.

Limontri furrowed his brows at the crown prince's unapologetic cheerfulness.

"I don't appreciate the attention," he grumbled.

In response, Hiel simply shrugged and said, "You sure do have a lot of complaints."

Violet watched the exchange of friendly banter between the crown prince and Limontri. She was feeling quite pleased with the outcome of the crown prince's recommendation.

Turning to grin at Aris, Hiel said, "My apologies, Lady Horissen."

Despite the words spoken, his attitude clearly reflected that he was the slightest bit apologetic—all Aris could do was join Limontri in glaring daggers at him.

Aris joined the crown prince in his carriage for the ride back to the palace. Since he had selected her as his Flower, the two would be together until they got back to the palace.

"I can't believe I'm in a carriage with you, Your Royal Highness," she said.

"So, how does it feel?" Hiel asked.

"It's tolerable."

Honestly, she wasn't thrilled in the slightest. The crown prince was always a perfect gentleman, but she knew he was still the type of man who was never honest with women.

"To be honest," Hiel started.

"Yes?"

"I didn't catch that boar."

Aris blinked in surprise. "Then it was Duke Essel?"

"No," Hiel said. Realizing what this implied, Aris' jaw dropped. Seeing the truth dawn on Aris' face, Hiel continued, "It's exactly as you think. Lady Essel caught it."

She'd heard that Violet was a decent archer, but to think she was talented enough to catch a wild boar!

"I don't feel great about it," Hiel admitted.

Aris tilted her head in confusion. "Why not?"

"Because I'm not the one who caught it," he said. "She only shared the boar with me so that I could be the center of attention today."

"I guess that's understandable."

Aris knew Violet had been traveling with Hiel, so she thought it unlikely that Violet had simply stumbled across the boar by herself. Rather, she assumed Hiel had been the one who discovered the boar, while Violet had shot it. And here she had said that she would only catch small game! Violet had probably suggested claiming the win as a team because she knew she would end up out hunting him.

"It was a wise decision on her part."

"Was it?"

"If she outshone you, it would reflect poorly on her," Aris said, nodding.

Hiel frowned at her statement. "I wouldn't harass others simply because they bested me."

"You wouldn't," Aris said, straightening her posture. She looked Hiel dead in the eyes. "However, the same couldn't be said for your supporters."

Nothing good could come of beating the crown prince. It was a foregone conclusion that everyone would naturally step aside to guarantee Hiel's victory in whatever he participated.

"If you were Violet, would you have claimed that boar for yourself?"

Hiel gaped at her, blinking dumbly.

"Anyone with half a brain would have made the same decision," Aris said, nodding.

She continued to be amazed by Violet's precociousness.

"I see."

Hiel appeared to be reflecting on what Aris said.

Aris glanced at the crown prince. "You should thank Violet. Genuinely."

"What?" Hiel asked.

"You're grateful, aren't you?"

Hiel's expression briefly faltered. "Why should I be?"

"If you weren't grateful, you wouldn't be telling me any of this right now."

"But—" Hiel started.

"And you feel apologetic towards Violet, don't you?"

At Aris' question, Hiel pursed his lips.

This man is never honest with himself.

Aris could tell that Hiel was grateful towards Violet, but his male pride made him hesitant to admit the truth. She smiled at his stubbornness.

"Why Limontri Raon, by the way?" Aris asked, changing the subject to lessen the awkwardness.

Hiel chuckled quietly. "He's a man with a personality like yours."

"What does that mean?" Aris asked.

"He's the type who won't make a big deal about what happened today."

"Ah."

So, her hunch had been correct. She wondered how Violet was faring at that moment. She couldn't wait to get to the palace and see her.

At that same moment, Limontri Raon was peering at Violet. A headache was forming at the thought of having to dance with her as soon as they reached the palace. What would his parents think? He continued to survey her, taking in her appearance. She was breathtakingly beautiful, even with her hair tied up and dressed in pants. However, she was also undeniably young.

"You will have to excuse me for a moment once we arrive at the palace," Violet said, breaking the silence.

"Is something wrong?" Limontri asked.

"No, I just need to change into my dress," she replied.

Everyone who had attended as a Flower was already dressed in their formal attire. Having sat indoors all day, there was little need to freshen up. However, that was not the case for the participants of the hunt.

"I see." The two fell back into silence. Limontri turned to Violet again, and asked, "Did the crown prince specifically tell you to pick me?"

Violet nodded in response. "He told me you wouldn't read too much into the situation," she said.

Limontri ran his hand through his hair and sighed. "I see."

In his head, he began plotting how to get satisfactory revenge on the crown prince. Hiel could not stand being alone; he always needed someone at his side. That was one reason he had started gathering mistresses. Limontri decided he would spurn the crown prince the next time he was asked to visit. Hiel could deal with his loneliness on his own. How could Hiel just throw him into this situation? He was a good friend, but he could also be a tremendous pain.

"I had to be careful who I chose," Violet murmured. "It would be troublesome if my partner mistook our dance to mean anything more than that."

Limontri understood Violet's concerns.

"Nothing like that will happen," Limontri laughed quietly. "I'm not the eldest, so I'm unlikely to inherit my family's title and estate. However, I have enough money to make it on my own. I won't try to leech off of you, my lady."

Violet felt a sense of déjà vu.

"Ah." She burst out in giggles, which made Limontri give her a curious look. "You're just like Big Sister."

"Pardon?" he asked, confused.

"Your personalities are quite similar. Big Sister always gets straight to the point, just like you," Violet replied.

"By Big Sister, are you referring to Lady Horissen?" Limontri asked.

"Yes, that's correct," Violet said, nodding. "I already feel close to you, since you're so alike."

Limontri furrowed his brows. He didn't particularly want Violet to enjoy his company. "Keep that closeness to yourself, please."

"Shall we become friends as well?" Violet asked. She could understand why the crown prince had sought to be friends with Aris.

"Excuse me?" Limontri scoffed in disbelief. "You're joking, right?"

"I'm quite serious," Violet responded.

"Men and women can never be just friends," Limontri said dryly.

"Big Sister and the crown prince are friends, too," Violet countered.

He was well aware of that. In fact, the crown prince had told him of his newfound friendship with Lady Horissen the day it happened. He'd mentioned that it'd be hard to spend a lot of time with her since she was a lady, but she was fun to be around. Still, he did not make friends with women.

"I must decline," Limontri said firmly.

Despite his stony rejection, Violet smiled. "Let's be friends. We can dance together when we see each other at balls."

"You say you want to be friends, but you're really just looking for a dance partner," he said coldly.

Violet vehemently shook her head in denial. "Well, I mean, that is part of the reason, but I truly would like to be friends with you!"

Seeing Violet still treating him with warmth and kindness even after he'd reacted harshly, Limontri's heart softened. "Well, I suppose we could have a cup of tea sometime."

"Oh my! That sounds wonderful!" Violet grinned.

She realized that her approach to Limontri was not unlike the way the crown prince had approached Aris.

It felt just like that.

The carriage finally arrived at the palace. Hiel alighted, followed by Aris. As she stepped outside, she rolled her shoulders and stretched her tense muscles.

"You should head over to the ballroom first. I'm going to go change," Hiel said.

All the hunters were rushing off to get dressed.

"Yes, Your Royal Highness."

Parting ways, Aris began walking towards the ballroom.

How pretty, she thought.

A chandelier sparkled and shone from the ballroom ceiling, the lamps hanging from the walls glowed prettily. Underneath the lights, people had begun to gather. Apart from the winners, a few other high-ranked hunters had also chosen some of the Flowers as their partners for the evening. The rest of the Flowers who remained unattached were gathering in a group, talking amongst themselves.

"Big Sister!" Violet exclaimed, as she entered the ballroom. Her blonde hair cascaded down her back, and she looked dazzling in her pale green gown. Limontri accompanied her at her side.

"Hello," Aris nodded in greetings towards Limontri. She hadn't been able to properly greet him.

"It's a pleasure to make your acquaintance, Lady Horissen." Limontri bowed his head in response.

"Please, call me Aris," she replied warmly.

"Alright, Aris," he responded.

The combination of his silver hair and crimson eyes was striking. Standing next to each other, Violet and Limontri made a handsome pair.

"May I ask how old you are?" Aris asked.

"I turned nineteen years old this year," Limontri responded.

That would make him the same age as the crown prince. There was a bit of an age difference, but he looked good with Violet. Violet needed a man who didn't have any political ambitions of his own, anyway. If Limontri was that kind of man, he surely would have sparked the younger girl's interest.

"Big Sister, we've decided to be friends," Violet gushed happily.

Why does it sound like she's talking about a potential husband?

Violet wasn't the type to offer friendship with just anyone. There was definitely another motive at play, and Aris was sure Limontri had his suspicions, as he made a face at the word friends.

"All I said was that we could have tea sometime…" Limontri trailed off.

"That makes the two of you friends," Aris said, ever on Violet's side.

Limontri was at a loss for words. He realized that no matter what he said, his words could be turned against him.

"Announcing the arrival of His Royal Highness!"

The winner of today's hunt, the crown prince, entered the room. Spotting Aris, Violet, and Limontri, he walked towards them slowly.

"Announcing the arrival of His Imperial Majesty!"

The emperor, the host of the Great Hunt, entered soon after. Following behind him were Louison and Ian.

Now that everyone had arrived, the ball could start. Those with partners made their way to the dance floor, and those without partners stood off to the side. Aris and Hiel began dancing as well. Aris had contemplated whether she should step on Hiel's toes, but let him off since he'd introduced Violet to a good partner.

"Don't step on my feet this time," Hiel warned, having already predicted her intentions.

"You knew?" Aris asked sweetly.

"Of course," he growled. "I only let it slide because it was you."

"I'm honored."

She didn't think she could get away with stepping on his toes anymore. It was unfortunate, but there was nothing she could do about it. They continued to dance, and as the music played on, Hiel gazed at her.

"Is there a man you're interested in?" Hiel asked.

Aris cocked her head at the sudden question. "Why do you ask?"

"As your friend, I'm curious what kind of man would catch your fancy."

Aris grinned at this.

Hiel was confused by her reaction. "Why are you smiling?"

"I'd be lying if I said there wasn't."

Her answer came as a shock. Hiel hadn't expected her answer and continued to fire off questions. "Is he better than me?"

Hiel, who held himself in the highest regard, seemed almost—how should she put it—cute to be asking such a thing. She shook her head. Truthfully, she wanted to respond that the man she fancied was better than Hiel, but there was no need to hurt his feelings.

"There aren't many men who can claim to be better than you. You have royal blood and possess impressive titles… but to answer your curiosity… he's simply a quiet man who respects women. That's why I'm waiting for him. Though, it's just a one-sided crush."

This Aris, who spoke with a wistful smile, seemed unfamiliar to Hiel. She had always smiled so cheerfully that Hiel would never have imagined she could make such an expression.

"A crush?" Hiel frowned. "You're my friend. I can't stand to see you sitting around and pining for someone. You're not just sitting around doing nothing, are you?"

Kkamang Kkamang

After the ball ended, Aris and Lucine finally made their way back home.

"I'm exhausted!" Aris exclaimed.

"Of course you are, my lady. You've been standing and dancing all night."

Lucine had applied facial oils to her hands and was diligently removing Aris' makeup. Aris recalled reading about magic like that in fantasy novels, where people could remove anything with a simple spell. Unfortunately, nothing like that existed in this world.

"I wish there was a way to remove all of my makeup with magic," she grumbled.

"That sort of thing doesn't exist," Lucine responded matter-of-factly.

"When will the rabbit Violet gifted us be cooked?" Aris asked.

"It will likely be served tomorrow," Lucine replied without pausing her hands.

Thrilled at the thought of a sumptuous feast, Aris disrobed and prepared to bathe. The bath prepared was mixed with milk, and rose petals floated on the surface.

"What's all this?" Aris asked.

"You'll turn seventeen soon, my lady," Lucine said. "You'll be needing things like this from now on."

Realizing what Lucine was implying, Aris blushed furiously. "You mean, I'll be old enough to get to know men intimately?"

"Yes," Lucine replied.

It was prudent to ensure Aris always smelled fragrant. Perfumes in spray bottles were good, but bath fragrances permeated the skin and the subtle fragrance would create a more elegant sense.

Lucine helped Aris into the bathtub quickly. "This is common for everyone. Let me know when you're finished."

"Okay," Aris said.

Most noble ladies had bath assistants that would bathe them, but Aris preferred to wash up on her own. She could never get accustomed to having others scrub her body for her. After she had cleaned and soaked her body, she got out and slipped on a robe.

When she exited the bathroom, Lucine steered her towards the makeup vanity, and said, "I'll dry your hair for you."

As Lucine went to task drying her hair, Aris suddenly remembered she hadn't written a letter that day yet. She asked Lucine to ready her stationery and pen, but Lucine suggested waiting till tomorrow instead.

"No, I want to write it before I sleep," Aris said, with a slight shake of the head.

After her hair had dried, Aris went into her room and sat at her desk.

Lucine entered with the stationery and the new wax stamp.

"How did you know I was going to use my wax stamp?" Aris asked.

"I could just tell," Lucine remarked.

Lucine really has an eye for this sort of thing, Aris thought, as she began penning the day's events to paper.

As always, she ended her letter stating she wouldn't need a reply. She took care in her manner of writing to avoid scaring him off. The letter was quickly sealed with a drop of melted wax and her crescent moon stamp. Aris felt pleased, thinking the stamped design turned out quite pretty.

"I'll send it tomorrow," Aris said, looking at the sealed letter.

"Get some rest now, it's been a long day," Lucine replied.

Once Aris was settled into bed, Lucine turned off the lights and left.

I hope reading my letter will bring a smile to his face.

She wondered what he thought about when he read her letters. Did he burn them? Did he even read them? These thoughts filled her mind.

I'll just send them, anyway.

If she kept sending them regularly, she was sure he'd respond someday. This, she thought with certainty as she drifted off to sleep.

After each battle, Roy always returned to his personal barracks. Other soldiers would go into town to blow off some steam with the company of women, but he never joined them. His men would talk about the wonderful smell of women and the feeling of their supple flesh, but he remained uninterested. He only wanted to experience it with a woman he truly loved. He had no intention of spending a night with someone for whom he had no feelings. Thurwin always complained he was being a prude, but Roy remained steadfast.

"Commander!" Thurwin said, approaching him. "Are you really not going to go?"

The superiors had allowed the troops to have the day off to themselves, and many were heading to town.

"What's the matter? You know I'm not," Roy said flatly. "Otherwise, bring me back a mute girl then."

"Jeez, really, Commander. You know I can't go if you don't," Thurwin grumbled, following Roy into his barracks.

Inside, the two men spotted something placed on Roy's desk.

"It's a letter!"

However, as they moved closer, it was clear the letter had been sent from Roy's friend who lived in the countryside.

"Lady Horissen hasn't written you a letter in a while, huh?" Thurwin remarked.

Roy turned to give Thurwin a pointed look. "Why are you bringing her up?"

Roy was disgruntled at Thurwin's words. It was as if he'd been caught secretly looking forward to her letters.

"Of course I should bring her up," Thurwin responded.

"Don't be stupid," Roy said, sitting down. He had expected the letters to stop coming since he'd never written her back.

Suddenly, there was a noise from outside, calling out, "Commander Roy, you have mail."

"What are the chances!" Thurwin exclaimed as he flung the door open.

A knight entered holding an envelope—it was made of pretty, pink stationery, and a delicate scent wafted from it. Not only was there a letter, but a bouquet had also arrived with it.

"Wow, it really came!" Thurwin said as he looked on expectantly.

Roy touched the letter carefully with a slight tremble.

Noticing his unusual mood, Thurwin said, "Ah, well, I'll take my leave now."

He quickly excused himself to give his commander some privacy.

Once he was alone, Roy opened the envelope.

Dear Sir Roy,

Apparently, she had attended the Great Hunt as a Flower of the Hunt and hadn't been pleased to have been selected as the crown prince's dance partner again. She also wrote that she approved of the man the crown prince had introduced to Violet. Her letter continued on, sharing a variety of stories with him, finally adding that the bouquet was a present and she didn't need him to send a response this time as well.

"A present, huh?"

He touched the petals of the dried bouquet. There seemed to be a light fragrance still coming from the flowers. It felt like Aris' existence was consistently knocking on the door to his heart.

A response—he glanced at his stationery and pens before shaking his head. This would probably be the last letter, he thought to himself, fighting back the urge to write back to her. He couldn't cave in. He had to make sure these feelings ended with him. Roy thought of the beautiful Aris Horissen, clenching his fist as he pictured her smile. If she sent him one more letter, he wasn't sure he'd be able to hold himself back. The moon design of the wax seal shined beautifully. He stroked the seal silently, feeling sad and a little sorry for himself.

War was exhausting. Roy was looking at Aris' letter, with her pretty, round handwriting lining the pages. Out of the corner of his eye, he could spot the bouquet she had sent as well. He held it close and inhaled a deep breath of its sweet floral scent. It was not a scent one could find on the battlefield. When he smelled the flowers, it almost felt like the war was ending.

"Aris Horissen," he muttered to himself, looking back and forth between the bouquet and the letter.

He felt a strange emotion well up inside of him. Roy wondered how it would feel to receive another letter, sighing as he imagined it. For all he knew, this past letter could have been his last. The mere thought of it filled him with sadness and dread. He felt as if he had become addicted to these letters.

Kkamang Kkamang

THE RESPONSE

Aris folded up her letter and smelled the paper with a smile. "I almost feel like a pervert," she muttered aloud to herself.

In a dream she had the night before, a man had appeared and kissed her letter. She knew instinctively the man was Roy, whom she'd been waiting for all these years. She wondered what Roy looked like in person. She'd seen portraits of him but had never seen him in the flesh. Neither had any of the messengers she sent.

This letter would be her fourth; almost half a year had passed since she started sending letters to him. It had been spring when she'd written her first letter, and now summer was on its last legs. Autumn was quickly approaching.

"My lady," Lucine said as she entered.

Kkamang Kkamang

With a resigned expression on her face, she watched Aris press her stamp into the melted wax on the paper before her. Aris was sending yet another letter. Despite having never received a response, nor knowing whether the receiver even read any of her letters, Aris steadfastly continued to send them. Lucine felt sorry for her sweet lady. She didn't understand what made Aris so insistent on this man when she obviously deserved so much more.

"What's the matter?" Aris asked.

It was the weekend, and Aris had no plans or tasks for the day. It was also Lucine's day off, so it was unusual for her to come to Aris' room herself.

"You've received an invitation to a party," Lucine said.

Aris declined most of her invitations for social events, as she didn't particularly enjoy attending balls and other social events. Her dislike didn't rise to the level of hate, but she preferred to avoid public appearances, as all eyes would inevitably be on her. Frequent outings increased the chances of people gossiping about her.

"Just decline it, as always."

"I don't think you'll be able to," Lucine said.

"Why not?"

"It's from the palace."

Aris' expression crumpled. The crown prince would never believe her if she tried to excuse herself due to illness. The two now regularly had tea together once or twice a month.

"When was the last time I went to the palace?"

"Two weeks ago."

"I guess it is time for me to visit," Aris said. She couldn't refuse when her friend had called on her.

"Oh dear," Lucine remarked. "I'm concerned about what you should wear."

"I still have plenty of dresses!"

Aris had purchased several summer dresses not too long ago. She'd outgrown her old dresses as she grew taller, and along with her height, her bust had also swelled in size, so new dresses were called for. Lucine had placed orders for new dresses a few months ago, but soon found it hadn't been enough.

"Everyone will be well dressed," Lucine said with determination. "It's my job to make sure you're dressed even nicer than usual."

After dancing with the crown prince twice, Aris' popularity had skyrocketed to where everyone in the capital knew of Lady Aris Horissen. Invitations poured in from people desperate to connect with Aris, who was widely considered to be the leading candidate for the title of crown princess. Lucine knew this well, and couldn't bear to let her lady go out looking any less than exquisite. The dresses she had purchased recently were flattering, but they weren't decent enough to wear to the palace. Why was it so difficult to find elegant dresses that bore just the right amount of skin?

"Honestly, my lady!" Lucine said with slight frustration. "You should be the one expressing concern on these matters to me!"

"Hm? Should I really?" Aris laughed.

"Of course!"

Usually, the request to be dressed in the latest fashions and trends came from the young ladies, and it was not uncommon for maids to be chastised by their ladies, who were unsatisfied with the results. Not once was this the case for Aris—she attempted to excel in everything, except for her appearance.

"I just want to see you dressed at your best," Lucine said seriously.

"I have faith in you, Lucine. You always dress me wonderfully," Aris responded.

"It's not that you trust me, it's just that you can't be bothered to do it yourself," Lucine complained, frowning at her lady.

Aris stuck out her tongue. "Oops, you caught me."

"Anyways, I'll reply to the crown prince's invitation that you will attend his tea party."

That was the real purpose Lucine had come in search of Aris; she needed to confirm whether Aris intended to accept the invitation.

Aris nodded her head. "Yes, I should attend."

She thought about the crown prince—he was the type that grew lonely easily. If she refused the invitation, he would surely be upset with her.

And to think he was such a jerk when I first met him.

Now, she couldn't help but think fondly about the boy she'd once despised.

Arrows were flying towards him from all directions. Roy, who had been shooting arrows atop a cliff, spotted the enemy captain amongst the approaching troops.

There he is.

The Empire of Oraan had suffered many losses during the war, but they refused to give up. Constant attacks were launched against the Xenonian troops hoping to turn the tide of war in their favor. This battle, like all others, was fierce. If things continued in this manner, the sporadic battles would soon explode into full-scale war.

Roy had once again strategized today's battle plans, first luring the enemy troops to the cliff, and then laying siege under a barrage of arrows. The plan had paid off nicely, with the enemy falling for the Xenonian army's tricks, and finding themselves entrapped at the cliff. Roy took aim at the enemy captain from afar and released his arrow. The arrow lodged itself squarely in the captain's throat. Roy was a skilled swordsman, but he was equally talented as a marksman. He had quickly earned the moniker of golden shot, and as an archer befitting his nickname, he had ended the captain's life with a single arrow.

Realizing their leader had fallen, the enemy troops fell into disarray. They knew that if they continued the battle, they would surely be shot and killed. One by one, their horses turned around and retreated, while those charging on foot quickly followed. However, unbeknownst to them, Xenonian troops were lying in wait toward their retreat. This was all within Roy's plan to completely finish off the Oraanian army.

"Commander," Thurwin said, as he approached, "Shall we head down too?"

The enemy leader had been eliminated and their troops had hastily retreated.

Their work was done.

"Get in formation to seal all exits," Roy shouted in response.

The soldiers began scrambling towards the creek, as commanded. They were to prevent the enemy from entering or escaping from any exit point.

"I don't have any blood on me today," Roy remarked absentmindedly.

A new general appointed from the emperor's court had recently arrived to take over as the battle supervisor. He'd taken a liking to Roy and had positioned him in the safety of the archery division atop the cliff, saying he didn't wish to see Roy dead.

"Do you think Lady Horissen sent a letter today?" Thurwin asked.

Lady Horissen had been sending letters every one to two months. Three had arrived, and half a year had passed since receiving her first letter.

"If she did, I would have received it already," Roy replied, as he always did.

"Oh, Commander," Thurwin sighed. "Isn't it about time you send her a response?"

"I will if I receive another letter," Roy said.

He had already decided to write back if he were to receive another letter that was scented like her.

"She'll be the first lady you ever respond to."

"Do you really think another letter will arrive?" Roy asked.

"Of course," Thurwin said as if stating the obvious.

"Jeez," Roy laughed at Thurwin's unshaken confidence.

"You read her letters often," Thurwin noted.

He'd noticed how the commander often reread Lady Horissen's letters, and the traces of a faint smile on Roy's face when he did so. That's all it took for Thurwin to recognize that Roy was expectantly waiting for Aris' next letter. The commander was always on edge on the battlefield, but his atmosphere softened when he read her letters. They were clearly special to him.

"You could tell?" Roy asked, surprised. "I do enjoy the letters," he admitted, "but that's all there is to it."

"Commander," Thurwin grumbled.

"It would be ill-advised to want more," Roy repeated adamantly.

It would be bad indeed, he repeated internally, as though to discipline himself.

No matter how beautiful she was, or how thoughtful and soothing her letters were to Roy, Aris' existence could never develop into anything more.

Soon enough, they could spot the barracks in the distance. Thurwin ran towards Roy's lodgings and looked at his desk. It was bare. There was no scented letter waiting for him.

"Not today, I guess," Thurwin said, disappointed.

Roy, who had followed a few steps behind him, smacked the back of Thurwin's head. "I told you not to be stupid."

Thurwin pouted. "Why am I being stupid?"

Thurwin quite liked Lady Horissen. Unlike others who'd written to the commander in the past, she had consistently continued writing to him without asking for anything in return. She even used scented paper and an elegant moon stamp to seal her letters. It was obvious a lot of thought went into each letter. To top it all off, she'd sent him a bouquet of dried flowers as well. Each of her actions had been a healing salve to the battered heart of a man at war.

Roy sat down at his desk. The flowers Aris had sent him were still laid on the side of his desk, as he had nowhere else to put them.

"Commander."

"What?" Roy asked.

"Do those flowers still smell nice?" Thurwin asked, pointing to the bouquet.

Roy nodded his head. "They've lasted quite long."

Unbeknownst to him, Aris had sent the flowers to a florist with a specialty in magic to be treated before she'd sent them to him, so the bouquet continued to maintain a subtle fragrance.

"Flowers that are treated with magic last for a long time," Thurwin remarked.

"I see." Roy paused. "I smelled them this morning."

"You like smelling flowers?" Thurwin asked, surprised.

The commander pretended not to care, but his actions really stated otherwise.

"When I smell them, it makes me feel like the war will be over soon," Roy said, holding the bouquet with one hand. He breathed in the smell of the blossoms and smiled. "They make me smile without realizing it."

"Sure, sure," Thurwin said, hastily leaving the room. He thought it best to leave Roy alone with his flowers.

Alone, Roy stroked the petals tenderly. He felt almost as if the flowers were smiling in his hands.

Lucine, having decided none of the dresses at home were satisfactory, had dragged Aris out to the shops.

"Come this way."

The designer ushered the two ladies in with a smile.

Aris and Lucine slowly strolled through the boutique. Inside, there were rows of beautiful dresses on display. Since there wasn't enough time to commission a dressmaker for a custom dress, the girls had come in search of an off-the-rack dress.

"This is pretty," Aris said, looking at one of the many gowns.

Lucine let out a hum of appreciation. It was obvious that the dresses on display had all been painstakingly crafted.

"How about this one?" Aris asked, pointing at another dress. It sported a low cut, and the shoulders were covered by a piece of sheer fabric.

"It's pretty," Lucine whispered. "You should try it on."

"Right?"

Aris glanced at the designer for permission to try on the dress.

"We can arrange a fitting for you, if you would like," the designer quickly responded.

Her potential client was none other than Lady Horissen herself! If word spread that Aris' dress was purchased from her boutique, all the leading families in the capital would flock to her for their dresses. She had designed a dress for Lady Horissen in the past, but Aris had selected another designer. It was a regrettable loss, so when she heard Aris was searching for a dress to wear to the crown prince's tea party, she immediately extended an invitation to her boutique.

The dress Aris had selected was a garment made with a specialized technique, and Aris looked splendid in it. The designer gazed at her with shining eyes.

"I'll take this one," Aris said decisively.

Even Lucine did not bother suggesting Aris try on other dresses; the one Aris had chosen looked resplendent on her.

"Excellent choice, my lady." The dress was fairly expensive, but the price was of little concern to the Horissen family. "We welcome your future patronage."

"We'll return in the fall," Aris said.

The dressmaker smiled brightly at Aris' response.

As she left the store, Aris glanced at her watch. It was still early—she'd expected it to take all day, but had found her dress at the first boutique, and now had time to spare.

"Should we head home?" Lucine asked.

Aris shook her head. "There's another place I'd like to visit."

"Where?"

"Over there," Aris said, pointing to a calligraphy store across the street.

Crossing the street, Aris began perusing the pens on display in the window as soon as she entered the store.

"Welcome," the shop owner said, greeting Aris and Lucine. He was stunned to see Aris in person, the young lady whose pictures were frequently featured in all the newspapers. "May I be of any assistance today?"

"What kind of pen would be suitable for a man?" Aris asked.

"How old is he?"

"He's in his twenties."

The shop owner was caught off guard. He hadn't expected her to be shopping for a present for a man. Hearing that the recipient was in his twenties, he deduced the gift wasn't intended for the crown prince. Despite brimming with curiosity, the shop owner sensibly remained professional.

"We carry pens from the Parker brand that may be suitable," he said.

He took out a pen and an inkwell—the pen lines were strong and clean, and the ink was a deep blue. It was modest in design, neither too flashy nor too plain. Aris picked up the pen to try herself and enjoyed feeling how smoothly the pen glided on the paper.

"Do you have other recommendations?" Aris asked.

"Most certainly," the store owner said, proceeding to show her a variety of other pens. However, none stood out to her as much as the first one.

"I'll take this one," Aris said, pointing to the first pen.

Her purchase was quickly wrapped, and they exited the store after settling payment.

"Are you planning to send that to him?" Lucine asked.

"Yes," Aris smiled. "Oh! I also need to buy a present for the crown prince too," Aris said, looking at Lucine expectantly.

"Honestly," Lucine nagged, "why don't you try paying as much attention to the crown prince as you do to that man?"

Lucine was exasperated that Aris invested so much time and effort into selecting a thoughtful present for Roy.

Aris shook her head. "I don't like thinking of the crown prince as a man," she replied.

Lucine knew Aris had a point. She sighed, remembering everything she'd read in the tabloids—she'd heard all the rumors of the crown prince's latest favorite mistress.

"What about gifting tea?"

"Tea?" Aris asked.

"Yes, something easy to drink."

The tea purchase was the last item on the agenda for the day. Luckily, there was a tea shop nearby. Aris entered and swiftly looked around the inside of the store.

"Welcome."

"Could you recommend a delicate tea for me, please?" Aris asked.

"Is this for a gentleman?" The store clerk inquired.

"Yes."

"How old is he?"

"He's in his late teens."

"This tea is the most popular with young men of that age." The clerk showed her a tea sample. It was priced towards the higher range, and the packaging looked elegant.

Aris paid for it with no hesitation.

"You really didn't think twice before buying that," Lucine said, as Aris exited the store.

"What?"

"It's just very different from when you were looking at pens earlier," Lucine remarked dryly.

"Well, that's because Sir Roy is…" Aris abruptly cut herself off. She felt like she revealed too much of herself to Lucine.

Roy is... the man I like.

Aris had thought long and hard about what to send Roy—it had to be something he wouldn't feel burdened to receive, but would still bring him joy. However, she'd intended for her efforts to remain hidden and hadn't wanted Lucine to notice.

"The crown prince is just a friend, that's why a simple present is best. If my present was too thoughtful, he'd interpret it the wrong way," Aris said.

"But Commander Roy is allowed to interpret it the wrong way?" Lucine asked sharply.

Aris' cheeks had flushed bright red, but when she responded with a resolute "yes", Lucine could only sigh. That man didn't spare her lady the time of day! Why was a lady as beautiful, sweet, and well-mannered as Aris hung up on a man like that?

Lucine supposed Roy had some decency—at the very least he wasn't a good-for-nothing who attempted to attach himself, like a leech, to a lady of Aris' pedigree, simply because she'd reached out to him first. Still, Lucine couldn't help but dislike him. Lucine continued to grumble to herself unhappily, but couldn't afford to stew for too long. Tomorrow was the day of the crown prince's tea party—there was still much to be done.

Aris woke up early the next day and received a massage before putting on her dress and getting dolled up. The pink flush of her cheeks looked lovely against her alabaster skin. When she had finished her preparations, Aris headed to the carriage. Her father had already left for the palace earlier that morning, so Lucine and Aris would ride the carriage together.

Lucine watched her young lady gazing at the scenery as they rode towards the palace, noticing how Aris was maturing by the day.

"I heard we're having tea in the Spring Garden again," Aris said, turning to face Lucine. Aris loved the Spring Garden—the crown prince knew this, and always made it a point to host the tea party there when she, along with other close friends, came to visit. Otherwise, the garden usually remained restricted for royalty. "Do you think Lady Violet was invited?"

"Probably," Lucine replied.

Aris hadn't asked, but it was likely that Violet and Limontri, who were also frequent guests at these tea parties, would be invited alongside her.

The carriage entered the gate reserved for nobles and pulled to a stop in front of the crown prince's residence, the Lion Palace.

Aris exited her carriage and noticed another carriage parked to the side. It appeared Lucine had guessed correctly.

"It's the Essel family crest," Aris remarked.

Lucine nodded and replied, "It looks like Lady Violet is here as well."

Aris made her way towards the Spring Garden, a short distance from the Lion Palace, while Lucine trailed close behind her. Soon, Aris found herself at the entrance of the Spring Garden and paused to take in the view with amazement. The flowers were in full bloom; their petals spread in splendor. Flowers that usually only grew in the springtime remained in bloom here—looking at the flowers, one might even think that time was at a standstill.

"I told you not to laugh."

She could hear the crown prince's voice coming from within.

"But it's hilarious."

The other voice giggled in response. The giggling voice belonged to Violet—it seemed like she had arrived early and was already sipping tea with the crown prince.

Aris wondered what was so funny that caused Violet to laugh without restraint.

Aris, curious what the two were talking about, approached quietly. However, she was spotted by Hiel as she neared them, and he turned and waved her over.

"Come join us, Aris,"

At their last tea party, she'd allowed the crown prince to drop the honorifics and call her by her first name. He'd taken to calling her Aris ever since.

"Big Sister, have you heard what happened to the crown prince?" Violet asked, still full of mirth.

"No, I haven't," Aris said, sitting down in an empty chair.

It seemed that she and Violet would be the only attendees of today's tea party with the crown prince.

"Last night, he didn't realize that his mistress had left, so he pulled one of his gentlemen-in-waiting into his bed and kissed him in his sleep."

"What? No!" Aris gasped.

How tired did he have to be to not realize that he was kissing a man?

Seeing that Aris had settled into her seat, Razaen approached her. "What would you care to drink?" he asked.

"Black tea, please," Aris replied.

Razaen bowed and left to prepare her tea.

A warm breeze blew—Aris chatted away with Violet and Hiel, sharing funny stories and discussing their concerns.

I could never dream of something like this in the real world.

Before the days she became Aris, she had been an orphan. Memories of her school life were filled with unhappiness—she recalled the constant bullying and the harassment by the boys in her grade. She grew wary of meeting new people; even boyfriends from past relationships never truly cared for her. She'd given up hope of ever finding a sincere friend to call her own. It would be apt to say that all her personal relationships had ended in failure.

And so, she learned to think in this manner:

I'm going to love myself, at the very least... and I'm going to find someone who truly loves me, and I'll spend my life with them.

She carried that conviction with her throughout her whole life. As she entered the final throes of cancer, she did whatever she pleased, and that had led her to this novel and the world she inhabited.

"Why are you smiling?" Violet asked.

"I'm just happy," Aris replied dreamily.

She was finally living alongside people who loved and cared for her. Her dreams had come true, and now she even dared to have another dream. A dream of happiness with Roy.

"By the way…" Hiel began, as he regarded Aris, "you mentioned there was a man you fancied."

"Yes, I did." Aris gave a slight nod and tilted her head.

"Who is he?" Hiel asked, unable to contain his curiosity.

Aris did not answer right away.

Hearing no response, Hiel continued to pry. "Is it a secret?"

"It's not that..." Aris said in a soft voice.

"If that's not it, then who is it?" Hiel demanded.

"Um, it's Sir Roy," Aris said simply.

"The Roy I know?" Hiel eyes widened. "The Roy that prefers mute girls?"

"Yes."

Why did he have to bring up that rumor?!

Aris felt flustered.

"I thought he'd at least be a count!" Hiel exclaimed.

He seemed uncharacteristically wound up, and his voice was getting louder. He had never expected Aris to harbor feelings for a commoner!

"Your Royal Highness. Calm down!"

"What?" He looked at Aris and laughed weakly. "Don't worry, I have no intention of getting in the way."

Still, he found it difficult to shake off his surprise.

"I can't believe you prefer him over me," Hiel said, as he ran his fingers through his hair. "Father was planning to grant him a title for his accomplishments in the war, but it won't come anywhere close to the Horissen family's prestige."

"I know," Aris said.

"You know that, and still—" The crown prince cut himself off. He could tell that Aris' feelings were genuine.

"I've been writing him letters," Aris added.

"Letters?"

"Yes."

"Has he replied?"

At this, Aris pressed her lips together and took a sip of her black tea.

"Why, I ought to!"

"I told him he didn't need to respond," Aris said calmly.

Even so, the nerve of him to not send a reply! How dare he! At his station? To ignore my friend?

Rage bubbled within Hiel, but there was nothing he could do or say. Aris insisted she was fine.

There was little need for a soldier to write on the battlefront. Even if he were to do so, the stories about his day were never sweet or endearing. Letters lay scattered across Roy's desk—these were all the letters he'd received from Aris. He'd thought there were more, but it was not the case. In actuality, she had only written to him a handful of times, but each letter had made a lasting impression on his heart. He considered them far too precious to be dismissed in the manner he'd dealt with letters he'd received from other ladies in the past. Why was that? What made this lady so special to him?

It was probably how she ended each letter saying that he did not need to write back to her. If she had asked for a response in her first letter, he probably would have penned a polite response requesting her to stop writing to him. He would have asked her to stop wasting his time. However, Aris was thoughtful enough to say she didn't expect a reply. It was as if she had read his mind. That's right—her letters were both exciting and amusing, and always ended with a brief note saying he needn't write back, taking his own thoughts and feelings into account.

I wonder if she did that on purpose — It was a thought he'd entertained often these days. If she had written her letters calculating his reaction, that meant the lady was a truly shrewd and formidable person. He would need to be on guard for those tricks. Yet, he hadn't detected any trace of deceit in the letters. The letters simply revealed the happy, quiet day-to-day events of a young lady.

Roy had never been present when the letters arrived, as he was often out on the battlefield. Instead, he would return to find a letter waiting for him placed on his desk. He wanted to hand his response directly to the messenger if he ever sent a reply, but knew he was unlikely to have that chance.

"Seems like it's time to respond," he muttered under his breath.

After half a year of receiving Aris' letters, Roy finally took out his stationery.

Dear Lady Horissen,

He paused, realizing he had nothing of worth to write about. He wasn't the talkative sort, like Thurwin. Eventually, he began quietly writing the day's events, but soon found himself stuck again on how to end the letter. He certainly couldn't tell her that he didn't expect a response as well...

"Commander!" Thurwin called out, as he entered without warning.

Roy tried to hide his letter in vain, but Thurwin had already noticed it.

"Ah!" Thurwin exclaimed.

"Announce yourself before you just barge in, won't you?" Roy growled.

"Were you writing a letter?" Thurwin asked.

"I was."

Thurwin cocked his head, then let his mouth fall open as realization dawned on his face. Excitedly, he asked, "Is it addressed to the young lady, by any chance?"

Thurwin recalled the commander had received a letter from one of his friends not too long ago, but by the way he was acting, it didn't appear he was writing to a friend.

"You're writing to the young lady, aren't you?" Thurwin repeated, his voice full of hope.

"Shut up." Roy's response was curt.

"I'm right, aren't I?!" Thurwin glanced at the paper sneakily.

The commander seemed embarrassed.

"Well, I did say I would write her back if she sent another letter," Roy said.

"She will," Thurwin said confidently. "She will, for your sake."

Thurwin was certain that the commander harbored feelings for the young lady. If the situation had been switched and the letters had been addressed to him, he certainly would. After all, she was a lady who sent fragrant letters into a violent war zone, writing consistently despite never having received a response, and she had even sent him presents too. Indeed, if Thurwin was the commander, he would no doubt have developed feelings for her.

"Why are you here, anyway?" Roy grumbled.

"The general is asking for you," Thurwin replied. "He wants to go for a drink."

"For me?"

The new general was a capable man, and Roy acknowledged his ability. However, his one fault was that he drank excessively. The general enjoyed celebrating the victories with a drink, and thanks to Roy and his string of successes, the general always had a bottle in hand.

"There might be a battle tomorrow," Roy said, clicking his tongue, before looking at his desk. "At least let me finish writing this first."

Roy poured his honest feelings into the letter before folding it neatly and placing it into an envelope. Exiting his barracks, he resolved to hand the letter over to the soldier in charge of the mail. As he walked, he wondered what Aris might think when she read his letter. This thought alone was enough to make his heart race.

Aris had a dream that night. In it, a man appeared before her and leaned to whisper in her ear.

"Thank you for the letters."

"Oh my…"

"I love you," he said.

Aris felt a wave of overwhelming sorrow wash over her. Being treated tenderly with love and care in her dreams only served to hurt more.

When she opened her eyes, it was already morning.

"Ah..."

Why did she have that kind of dream?

"Maybe I'm a little starved for affection," she murmured to herself.

She had originally sent the letters with only the intention of friendship, but her feelings were strayed in another direction.

"We're going to get married anyway, so it doesn't matter whether I receive a response now."

She hadn't expected the crown prince would make such a big deal about it. She recalled what the crown prince had told her yesterday.

"Stop wasting your time. If a man isn't responding to you, it means he's not interested."

"But still…" Aris muttered to herself.

Roy had a rigid personality. He always followed through once he set his mind to it. If he really disliked her letters, he would have put a stop to them, requesting her to refrain from sending any more letters. She stared at the pen set sitting on her desk. The pen and inkwell had been packaged nicely inside a paper box. She wondered what Roy would think when he received it; she hoped it'd be to his liking. It was a far more practical present than the flower bouquet she'd sent last time, so she hoped he wouldn't reject it and would put it to good use instead.

It will be his birthday soon.

Roy's birthday was in the fall. It was much later in the year than Aris' birthday, which was in late spring.

"He probably has no idea when my birthday is," Aris sighed. Still, she'd secretly hoped that he might surprise her with a birthday present.

Let's be realistic.

He was a man who was constantly engaged in battle. Aris smiled brightly, as she felt herself returning to her usual cheerfulness. A gloom had settled in after listening to Hiel's misgivings, but she managed to bounce back in no time.

"My lady, you're up early," Lucine said, bringing over a basin of water for Aris to wash her face.

"Good morning, Lucine."

Aris freshened up and patted her face dry with a towel.

"The marquis is calling for you," Lucine said.

"Father is?"

Was something the matter? She hadn't heard of any upcoming events in the palace. Aris hurried over to the main house, wondering what could possibly be the matter. There were guards stationed outside the study, as always, and they opened the door for Aris when she arrived. Ian had not been called to the palace today and was working inside his study.

"Father, I've arrived."

"Ah, you're here," Ian said, smiling. From his expression, it didn't seem like there was anything troublesome. "The emperor has invited you as a guest to his vacation residence."

"Vacation residence?" Aris asked, perplexed. "Why me?"

"Yes, well…" Ian knitted his brows together. "He said that he wished to speak with the future crown princess."

The emperor had mistaken Hiel and Aris' friendship for something more.

"He was joking, of course," Ian quickly added.

"If I go, will I have the chance to speak with the emperor?" Aris asked.

"You can."

The emperor would host this party himself. It was a chance for him to speak with people of importance and spend time with them. Invites were usually extended only to bureaucrats and nobles, but Aris had received a special invitation.

"Violet will be there as well," Ian said.

"Ah." Aris nodded. At least she would have company.

"Also," Ian said, before pausing.

"Yes, Father?"

"Did you ever receive a reply?"

Aris felt her face grow hot at her father's unexpected question. "You knew?"

"It's been happening under my roof. I've known that you've been writing to Roy for quite some time now."

"Ah." She shook her head dejectedly. "I have yet to receive a reply."

"That's good."

"Pardon?" Aris lifted her head in surprise.

"If he was a man who'd chase after you for our family's wealth, I would have eliminated him already," Ian responded.

Aris opened her eyes wide. "Did you investigate Sir Roy's background?"

"Naturally."

Her father's unabashed response left Aris at a loss for words.

"Would you like to view the results?" Ian asked.

"No, thank you."

If there was anything she wished to know, she'd ask him herself. She had no interest in learning about him by digging through his past.

"Aris," Ian said, "you are a beautiful young lady. Sometimes, useless pests will try to latch onto women like you."

"So, what is Sir Roy?" Aris asked, her eyes glinting. She was curious about her father's assessment of him.

"He's a very determined and extremely capable young man. He's achieved much more than he's received credit for." However, it was a far more difficult matter to determine whether he was a kind man. "There are no records of past relationships, so I cannot speak to how he treats women."

"Ah."

Aris held herself back from defending Roy's moral character. She couldn't exactly explain to her father that she knew this because she was aware of what would happen in the future. At any rate, she now found herself presented with a chance to meet with the emperor. This would be an excellent opportunity for her.

"Father," Aris said, "what type of woman does the emperor prefer?"

"What? Aris, by any chance..." Ian's face paled. "Do you want to be the empress?"

It was said that the empress was extremely beautiful, and Juselle had dearly loved her. Even when she passed away after giving birth to the crown prince, he never re-married after her death. Ian couldn't shake his nervousness at Aris' unexpected interest.

"Father, what would possibly make you think that?" Aris shook her head vehemently.

"This is the first time you've asked me about another man's taste in women. I can't help but worry," Ian replied.

"I just wanted to look nice when I greet the emperor," Aris said quickly to quell her father's fears. It wasn't entirely true though—Aris had an ulterior motive. "Really, that's all it is."

Convinced, Ian nodded, and said, "The emperor prefers a woman who exudes modesty. The empress always pinned her hair up and wore modest dresses."

Aris nodded and smiled—so that's how she would have to dress. It had been a long time since she'd dressed up for someone else. Lucine would definitely wonder what she was plotting this time, but Aris had no intention of sharing her plans with anyone. If Lucine knew of her goal, she would certainly disapprove.

"A modest dress?" Lucine questioned.

"Yes," Aris said with a grin.

"Should we have you fitted for a new one?" Lucine wondered aloud. Aris' wardrobe consisted of only low-cut dresses that were in vogue; it would be difficult to find demure-styled dresses.

"What about this one?" Aris pointed to a dress she'd never worn before. It was a yellow dress with a high neckline that would cover her decolletage. Pleats were gathered around the neck and exuded a sense of modesty and sophistication.

"This dress is…" Lucine trailed off.

"I know," Aris said softly.

It was a dress that had belonged to her late mother. That was one reason Aris had never worn it before.

"The style is a bit dated."

"That's why the emperor will appreciate it," Aris replied.

Aris had a valid point. Lucine took the dress out of the wardrobe and helped her into it—the result was quite stunning; Aris looked extremely elegant in the dress. It was a style normally worn by adults, but it looked amazing on her.

"You really have an air of maturity," Lucine said. "To think you can even pull off dress styles like this."

Aris supposed she could pass for an adult. She had only just turned seventeen, but passersby on the street almost never viewed her as her age.

Aris gathered her hair together and twisted it up, revealing her milky white neck. "I'd like to go with an updo."

"Why are you even trying to dress up for the emperor?" Lucine asked.

Aris had no interest in the emperor; she had no interest in any man other than Roy. Lucine thought it was strange that Aris was suddenly so invested in her appearance.

"Are you plotting something?"

"No," Aris quickly refuted, as if she had no idea what could've possibly given Lucine that idea.

Lucine, unconvinced, continued to eye her suspiciously, but Aris kept her expression blank. Resigned to the fact that her lady would never be easy to read, Lucine changed the subject, and asked, "Will Lady Violet be attending as well?"

"Yes," Aris said, to which Lucine sighed.

"What's the matter?" Aris pried.

"Even if you were dressed in the latest styles, it still might not be enough to compare, but to be dressed in an antiquated dress, I worry it isn't the prudent choice."

"Even if I were to wear the most stylish clothes, it won't matter unless the emperor likes them," Aris said with a smile, before turning back to the mirror.

Lucine experimented with a few different hairstyles on Aris so they could decide what looked best.

She smiled. "I guess it doesn't matter if the dress is old-fashioned since you're so pretty to begin with, my lady."

"Quit flattering me!" Aris chided Lucine playfully.

When Lucine retorted that she was being serious, Aris couldn't help but smile. It was a smile that made everyone around her happy.

The emperor studied his reflection in the mirror. His long blond hair was tied at the base of his neck, and he was dressed in black formal military dress. It suited him well.

"I'm a pretty handsome fellow," he murmured, glancing at the mirror. "If only my wife could be here to see this."

As he thought about his late wife, he finished his preparations. There was a knock on the door, and the door opened to reveal Hiel. His son was dressed in similar black military garb, and looked dashing as always.

"Are you ready, Father?" Hiel asked, as he entered the room.

"I don't know who you take after, but you're pretty easy on the eyes," Juselle said playfully.

"Obviously," Hiel said boldly, before pausing to look at his father.

"Is there something on your mind?" Juselle asked.

Hiel seemed to think for another moment before speaking. "It's about Roy."

"Ah, the commander?"

"What are your impressions of him?"

It was the first time Hiel had ever expressed an interest in another man.

Juselle grinned widely, flashing his teeth. "Are you curious?"

"Yes."

There was an ongoing conflict with the Oraanian Empire, but Xenon remained at peace. That was how successful Roy had been at containing the war outside their borders. Despite Oraan having issued a declaration of war, its impact had not permeated down to the people of Xenon. All of this was thanks to Roy.

"People who are being hailed as heroes participated in the war zone that Roy is stationed at. It seemed suspicious, so I did some investigation," Juselle said.

"And?"

"The results were interesting."

"What happened?"

Juselle tilted his head. "Why the sudden interest in him?"

"Ah, that... I have my reasons."

The reasons involved Aris, but Hiel couldn't tell his father that.

"Those so-called heroes had taken credit for Roy's contributions," Juselle said.

"I'm sorry?"

"The feats were all executed by Roy."

It was shocking. Roy had practically been fighting the entire war single-handedly. Where did a man of this caliber appear from? Juselle immediately began looking into his past. Roy had gained notoriety ever since his days at the academy. He was known to be outstanding in both hand-to-hand combat and strategy, but particularly excelled in sword fighting and archery. On top of his excellent prowess, he did not waste time on women or alcohol. Juselle had caught wind of the rumors surrounding Roy before, but had always assumed they were greatly exaggerated. However, after digging into his background, he was impressed to find Roy was even more extraordinary than the rumors described.

"All of those achievements are his?" Hiel was astonished—if that was true, then Roy was too perfect. He would certainly be envied and hated by the men around him. "Good heavens!"

"Yes. The interesting thing is Roy hasn't raised a single word of protest. Even when others steal his credit, he doesn't complain or argue."

"And?"

"That's how he's avoided making enemies of the men jealous of him."

It meant that Roy was a man who knew how to survive in society. How did Aris discover a man like him? Did she send him letters because she'd recognized how accomplished he was?

"Father."

"What is it?"

"Have you finalized the guest list for the New Year's Ball?" Hiel asked.

In the empire of Xenon, a ball was always hosted on the first day of the new year at the palace. All the noble families and distinguished figures in each field were extended an invitation.

"I will soon," Juselle said.

"I would like you to extend an invitation to Roy as well."

"Oh?"

You'll have to meet him at some point, won't you?"

"Hmm." Juselle considered the proposition and nodded. "It's about time we bring him home from the war."

It was unwise for one person to be in charge of too much. Juselle needed to ensure that the military could function with or without Roy. He had played too large of a role in the current war with the Empire of Oraan; if this continued for too long, the troops could not fight without him.

"I would like to meet him sometime," Hiel added.

It seemed that Hiel had a particular interest in Roy. Juselle wondered why he was so insistent on meeting him, but based on his son's attitude, it didn't seem like Hiel would divulge his reasons. Hiel was an excellent keeper of secrets—if he remained silent, he would take it to the grave.

Well, Juselle thought, *I'll figure it out, eventually.*

"Let's be off then," Juselle said.

The two departed and headed to the carriage that was waiting to take them to the vacation residence.

The flowers blanketed one section of the garden in a dazzle of colors. Those who had arrived at the vacation residence were scattered around, either sitting together in their cozy seats or standing and sipping their drinks. The heat from the summer day was slowly fading away. The slight chill of the evening was descending, carrying with it the faint scent of autumn.

Under the darkened sky, a carriage came to a stop. Aris, hair pinned up and donning a modest dress, stepped out of the carriage. Everyone's attention gathered on her. Aris made her way through the crowd of guests and surveyed the array of beverages. As a result of her recent diet, Aris had slimmed down significantly. As long as she maintained her current figure, Lucine could afford to be more relaxed with restricting Aris' diet. Seeing Lucine nod her permission, Aris happily sipped on her drink, and watched as another carriage arrived.

The carriage bore the crest of the Essel family. Aris expected to see Violet exit when the door opened, but to her surprise, a young man alighted first.

Isn't that Limontri?

Limontri Raon had exited Violet's carriage, and turned back to offer his hand to Violet as she stepped out.

How did this happen!?

Aris was burning with curiosity—to think that Violet would arrive with an escort!

Violet had spotted Aris from afar and walked towards her, Limontri following a few paces behind. "Big Sister!"

"Why did the two of you arrive together?" Aris asked.

"My father told us to."

"Oh my," Aris said, her eyebrows raised.

Limontri furrowed his brows. "It doesn't mean anything." He seemed concerned that arriving together might lead to mistaken speculation regarding their relationship. "I couldn't decline a request from His Excellency."

"I think His Excellency might've suggested it'd be fine if it was to mean something," Aris conjectured.

Aris knew better—the duke wouldn't request this of just any man. It appeared he approved of Limontri, seeing as he was attempting to connect the two. At her remark, Violet blushed furiously while Limontri scowled and sighed.

"You're right, he did say that. But Limontri and I are just friends," Violet explained.

Aris thought back to her own father—now that she thought about it, he'd known about her letters to Roy all along, but hadn't requested her to stop sending them. Maybe her Father approved of Roy, just like Duke Essel approved of Limontri!

"If things work out between the two of you, you should thank the crown prince," Aris teased.

"We don't have that kind of relationship yet," Limontri responded.

Aris smiled mischievously. "Yet?"

"Don't twist my words,"" Limontri groused. He avoided Aris' question and went to stand next to Violet.

Limontri claimed he didn't enjoy these social functions and that he'd been practically forced to attend, but would he really have come if he didn't harbor some feelings for Violet? At least, that was what Aris believed. Limontri was far less tolerant of others than she was. However, seeing as he always showed up for Violet, it seemed that he really treasured her as a friend, or possibly more. Only time would tell.

"Big Sister, your dress is quite modest today."

"Isn't it?"

"It suits you though," Violet said sweetly.

She was adorable, as always. She had recently turned fourteen, and the air about her seemed different somehow.

"Well, today's a special day," Aris said, smiling.

"A special day?" Violet couldn't decipher Aris' cryptic response.

"Yes."

"Announcing the arrival of His Imperial Majesty, the emperor!" a guard announced.

The star of the evening had finally arrived. A second announcement followed shortly.

"Announcing the arrival of His Royal Majesty, the crown prince!"

The emperor and the crown prince soon appeared side by side.

Hiel surveyed the crowd of attendees and saw his friends standing together. Even as he greeted other people, he kept glancing in their direction. At last, they began approaching. Aris, Violet, and Limontri greeted Juselle.

"Lady Horissen."

"Yes, Your Imperial Majesty?"

"You look quite lovely today," he said, gazing at Aris' outfit.

It was almost as though the empress had come back to life. Aris did not resemble the empress physically, but there was an air about her that reminded him of his late wife. Perhaps it was her choice of a modest dress paired with an updo, which was a style the empress had favored.

"Thank you," Aris said, curtsying deeply.

Juselle wanted to praise her excellent etiquette. He'd heard that Hiel and Aris were good friends. He supposed many couples started out as friends.

Once everyone had offered their greetings to the emperor and the crown prince, the music began to play. Like clockwork, Hiel sought out Aris for the first dance. Aris had long become accustomed to giving up her first dance to Hiel, and no longer made a face when he approached her; she simply began to dance with an air of resignation.

"You seem different today," Hiel said, taking in Aris' appearance.

"I do?"

"You don't usually wear clothes of this style."

He was right. Aris normally wore dresses that bared a little skin; it was rare to see her completely covered up. She reminded him of his mother as soon as he spotted her. They were not physically alike, but there was a similar aura. It was as if the image of his mother had come to life from the paintings he'd seen.

"It's similar to the empress' dresses, isn't it?" Aris grinned. Seeing Hiel nod, Aris looked pleased and said, "Then I've succeeded."

"What are you scheming?" Hiel asked.

"I wished to look nice for the emperor."

"Why are you trying to impress my father?"

"You'll see," Aris responded mysteriously, as she danced.

When the music ended, Aris retreated into a corner. She had fulfilled her duty and wanted to eat something delicious. Violet, who had also finished dancing with Limontri, soon joined her.

"Big Sister."

"Did you dance?" Aris asked.

"Yes!"

After his dance with Violet had ended, Limontri had immediately been surrounded by young ladies. As there weren't many ladies present that night, it wasn't necessary to split into partners. However, while women could decline a dance with someone, men could not. It was considered impolite for a man to turn down a young lady. The crown prince had also begun dancing with another lady, while several more were lining up for the chance to dance with the crown prince.

"Limontri is popular, isn't he?" Aris remarked, as they watched Limontri on the dance floor.

"His popularity probably increased after he danced with me."

Violet was right. After she had chosen Limontri at the Great Hunt, he had even been featured in the newspapers.

"By the way, Big Sister. Why are you dressed like this today?" Violet asked, curiosity coloring her tone.

"I wanted the emperor to be reminded of the empress when he looks at me," Aris replied.

At that moment, Aris noticed the emperor had been standing by himself after his first dance. Excusing herself from Violet, she began walking towards him.

"Your Imperial Majesty."

Juselle looked at Aris, who stood before him beneath the twinkling lights. She looked nothing short of pristine.

"Is there something you need?" he asked.

"May I request a dance?"

"Hmm."

Juselle did not dance with young ladies—if he ever danced, his partners were either married or a close friend of his. However, Aris had chosen to dress in a style reminiscent of the empress, as if she'd selected her attire to suit his tastes. Nor did it seem like she held any unsavory intentions.

"Did you dress up like that for me?"

"Do you like it?" Aris said, not denying anything.

Juselle smiled. "I do."

He granted her the dance in return for her efforts and held his hand out to Aris. The two began swaying to the rhythm of the music. Aris looked up at Juselle, who was leading her confidently across the dance floor.

"What did you need to ask of me?" Juselle asked.

Aris smiled brightly at the emperor's question. Her smile was as warm and infectious as always, and he couldn't help but return it.

"There's someone I wish to marry," Aris said.

"What?"

Juselle had been under the impression that things were going well with her and the crown prince, but it seemed that she had someone else in mind.

"Who is it?"

"It's Commander Roy," she answered honestly.

"Roy? You mean…"

"I'm referring to the man you're thinking of."

The crown prince had just asked him about Roy earlier that day as well. Juselle realized why he'd expressed such curiosity about the commander—it was because of Aris. Hiel had probably requested an invitation for Roy to the New Year's Ball for Aris' sake as well.

"You will need someone like me someday, Your Imperial Majesty," Aris smiled sweetly. "A young lady with power and status, who is from a family that's loyal to the crown."

Aris knew the emperor to be a highly calculating man. That was why he had married Roy into the Horissen family in the original novel. The time had not come yet, but it would eventually. When that time came, the emperor would have to find a suitable young lady.

"Someone like you?" Juselle chuckled. "Is this a prophecy?"

"When the time is right," Aris said, looking into the emperor's eyes. "I would like to ask you to keep me in consideration."

"Hmm."

"I fit all the requirements, and I will be waiting."

The emperor burst into a round of hearty laughter. Aris was being insolent, but he found the way she calmly presented her thoughts endearing. Even though she was close with the crown prince, she did not desire the title of crown princess. She had no grand ambitions, save for the goals she set for herself.

"Do you have any kind of relationship with him yet?"

Aris shook her head. "Things can change in the future."

Juselle nodded. "I see. I will remember what you've said to me today." He looked again at Aris appreciatively, before muttering to himself, "Most young ladies these days lack elegance. The empress was such a refined woman."

He pitied the young women decked out in the latest fashions, who approached him with dreams of becoming the next empress. They simply weren't his cup of tea.

"Thank you for allowing me to speak with you."

"The pleasure was mine," Juselle replied.

As the song drew to an end, Aris bowed her head and left the dance floor. She'd succeeded in conveying her intentions to Juselle. Roy would accomplish a great feat for the empire in the future. Having rejected a formal title, the emperor would order him to marry a young noblewoman. That woman would be no other than Aris Horissen

It's not time yet—Roy was still working through his smaller contributions to the war. His greatest achievement was still yet to come, but Aris couldn't just wait around until then. And so, she had taken the gamble and revealed her hopes for the future to the emperor.

He won't command me to become the crown princess anymore, will he? she thought as she walked away.

Suddenly, she spotted her father, who'd arrived after finishing his work at the palace.

"Father!" Aris called out joyfully.

"Aris," Ian said, strolling over to her.

"When did you arrive?"

"Just now."

"Ah, you should give your greetings to the emperor first."

"I will."

Ian headed towards the emperor and extended his greetings. Tired from his dance with Aris, the emperor was resting and enjoying a refreshing beverage.

"Ian."

"Yes, Your Imperial Majesty?"

"Your daughter told me she likes Roy."

Ian choked. "So, she did."

"Were you already aware?" Juselle asked.

"I was."

Juselle noted Ian didn't seem to be as overprotective of Aris as he usually was.

"He seems like an upstanding young man," Ian added.

Juselle furrowed his brows. "And my son isn't?"

"He's a heartbreaker," Ian retorted without hesitation. Juselle had little to offer in response. "You had mistresses too, Your Imperial Majesty. It made for quite a sticky situation when you met the empress later, didn't it?"

After meeting the empress, Juselle had become a loyal, loving husband, but he, too, had his share of dalliances during his youth. It was for that reason the empress had rejected him when they first met. The emperor had to work hard to change her mind. How often had Juselle gone to Ian with his problems when he was courting the empress? Ian recalled those days as he looked over at Hiel. The crown prince was engaged in conversation with Aris, Violet, and Limontri.

"I worry that the crown prince will also face the same difficulties," Ian said, looking at him pointedly.

Juselle remained at a loss for words.

Ian smiled. "He takes after you, Your Imperial Majesty."

"Which means?"

"He's a Casanova," Ian responded frankly. "He's not the one for my daughter."

"Your daughter told me that there would come a time when I would need her."

"Did she really?" Ian had no idea that Aris would say something so bold to the emperor. Out of the corner of his eye, he saw her making a face at something the crown prince had said. "I'm still looking into that man."

"Oho."

"If he's not fit for my daughter, I will make sure that she gives up on him immediately."

Ian was just watching for now, since his daughter seemed to like the man so much. However, if he caught so much as a hint that Roy might be an unsavory character, he would use his authority as her father to end their correspondence. Of course, Roy had yet to give him a reason to do so. He was just a regular soldier; one that didn't waste his time idling away with women like many soldiers did. He had scored a fair number of points with Ian for that alone.

"It would be best for Aris to remain good friends with the crown prince," Ian said.

That's the best decision for my daughter, Ian thought as he took a sip of his wine.

"Aren't you thinking too little of my son?" Juselle grumbled.

"I'm just speaking as a man with a daughter," Ian deflected, as he watched Aris smile. All he wanted was for her to be happy.

The party had ended, and Aris had managed to convey everything she wished to the emperor.

Awaking from a good night's sleep, Aris rubbed her eyes and sighed. That man had appeared in her dreams again—this time, he held her close in his arms, and softly whispered to her, *"I hope you like my letter."*

"I'd have to receive a letter first to have an opinion on it," she grumbled, taking out her prepared letter and present from her desk.

"Are you up?" Lucine asked as she walked in.

"Call Hiun in here," Aris said.

"Hiun? Are you sending a letter?"

"Yes." Aris replied.

Hiun had promised to deliver her letters whenever needed, and Aris always rewarded him handsomely in return.

"You should wash up first."

Aris agreed, and Lucine brought over a basin of water for her to wash up. After Aris had scrubbed her face and brushed her hair, she sat down on the sofa.

Soon, Lucine ushered in Hiun.

"Come in," Aris said.

"Yes, my lady."

"There are more items this time, so I'll pay you double. Be careful with them, alright?"

"Yes, my lady," he bowed.

He already received a generous payment, but now his lady was promising him two times his normal pay! Hiun was thrilled.

"It's a letter and the package is a pen and ink set," Aris said.

"Hmm. It might have to be inspected," Hiun said honestly.

Inspections at the battlefield were common for packages, and there was a chance that the package Aris had painstakingly wrapped might be ripped apart.

"That's fine. Tell them they may open the packaging if needed. Come back safely."

"Yes, my lady."

Hiun was relieved the young lady wasn't upset that the package might be opened before it reached Roy. He accepted the letter and the gift box and quickly left the room.

"Do you think he'll respond this time?" Lucine asked.

"I'm just glad he hasn't asked me to stop writing to him. If my letters made him uncomfortable, he could easily ask me to stop." Aris shrugged and clasped her hands together. "It'll be autumn by the time he receives the letter."

She hoped with all her heart that the letter would reach him safely.

Survival was the most important thing during times of war. It was important to survive on the battlefield, but it was also important to survive under the watchful eye of the generals. Roy stared at his glass. His superiors never forced him to drink, as he'd insisted that he didn't drink alcohol, but the other soldiers were not so lucky.

The Xenonian government was taking the war with Oraan seriously, and had sent over a distinguished general to the battlefield. General Risak Ren Zioden — Duke Zioden himself—had personally come down to the war zone. Since his arrival, Roy found himself consistently placed in the safest positions during battle. This resulted from Risak's protection.

"Roy."

"Yes, Your Excellency."

"How do you think tomorrow's battle will go?"

The Oraanian Empire had suffered a blow to their military efforts in the last battle, but they would soon return with more men and weapons.

Roy looked hesitant. "I'm not sure."

"So, there are things that even you don't know," Risak drawled.

"I don't know everything."

He was being honest; there was no way to know which direction the enemy would attack from.

As Risak lifted his glass to take another swig of his drink, Roy stopped him. "You're drunk, sir."

"Am I?"

"We might be needed on the battlefield tomorrow," Roy said gravely.

If Risak couldn't join the battle tomorrow because he couldn't wake up, it would mean big trouble. Criticism might even be directed at Roy for not managing his superior. Risak would come to his defense, of course, but it was best to avoid unnecessary trouble.

"You're too careful," Risak said, but set his glass down anyway. Nothing bad could come of listening to Roy. "Did I have too much to drink?" Risak glanced down at this glass.

"I think so."

All of the soldiers around them were tipsy, but only Roy remained sober. Risak hadn't indulged so much as to have lost his grip on reality, but any more and he'd certainly find himself in a state of inebriation. Roy, realizing this, encouraged him to stop.

"When are you ever going to have a drink?"

"When the war is over," Roy replied.

"That's too far off," Risak laughed softly. "When do you reckon the war will end?"

"This war has been lengthy, but don't you believe it will end soon?"

"Do you really think that?" Risak asked Roy.

"I need to hold on to that bit of hope in order to persevere."

Roy knew past events proved otherwise. As long as the Oraan empire held onto their greed, the war would rage on. He wondered how long his successes could continue. Sooner or later, his luck would run out and the foes of his past would come back to attack him. He had to leave the battlefield before that happened.

"You're not married yet, are you?" Risak asked.

"That's correct."

"What about a sweetheart?"

"He has one," Thurwin piped up.

Risak frowned. "Who is she?"

"Lady Aris Horissen."

"What?" Risak couldn't hide his shock.

Aris Horissen was the only daughter of the Horissen family. Despite only holding the title of Marquis, their influence rivaled that of a Duke. Not only did the emperor favor the Horissen family, Aris was also one of the crown prince's closest friends.

"They write to each other."

Thurwin's words came as a surprise to the general.

Roy pinched the bridge of his nose in exasperation.

"Is this true?" Risak asked.

Roy smacked Thurwin's head. "We're not in a relationship."

"But the letters, that part is true?"

"That's correct."

"Ah, what a shame," Risak said, taking a sip of water. "I was going to introduce you to a nice lady."

However, the household he had planned on introducing Roy to paled compared to the Horissen's. To think that the young Lady Horissen already sought out Roy! It seemed she was actively investing to secure her future.

"Ah, thank you for your consideration," Roy replied awkwardly.

This hadn't been the first time that the General had suggested introducing him to a woman. Roy could have declined as usual, but Thurwin's sudden declaration had complicated the situation.

"Well, I'll head back now," Roy said, standing up.

"We should all call it a night," Risak announced, bringing the night's festivities to a close.

The rest of the tipsy soldiers stood up teetering unevenly. Roy was the only one still sober. The men around him directed curious stares at Roy. Many were bursting with questions for him, especially after Lady Horissen had come up in conversation, but Roy remained silent as he returned to the barracks.

Thurwin followed close behind.

"You said something unnecessary back there," Roy grumbled.

"Oh, Commander. They were trying to set you up with another woman, of course I had to mention it."

"I can handle it on my own."

"I know you can, but…" Thurwin didn't think he was in the wrong. The commander already had a future bride. "I was just thinking of the lady of your house, that's all."

"The lady of my house?"

"Don't you think highly of Lady Horissen?"

That he did.

Roy exhaled a long sigh. "I don't harbor any special feelings for her."

"Are you sure?" Thurwin asked pointedly. "Can you honestly say that you don't have any feelings for her?"

"Thurwin."

"You're a coward, Commander."

Maybe Thurwin was right. Maybe he was a coward. Maybe he was afraid because he was uncertain how she'd react if he approached her.

"I should have been the one drinking tonight," Roy sighed.

"Commander."

Thurwin watched his commander push down his emotions. He appeared sad, maybe even pitiful.

"It's pleasant waiting for the letters."

"Commander."

"That's all," Roy repeated firmly.

That's all that it could ever be, he repeated to himself like a mantra, as he looked up at the night sky. A crescent moon hung low in the sky, just like the one in the stamp Aris used. The autumn breeze blew a chilly gust that swept through Roy's long hair.

"You should head inside now."

"I will."

Thurwin took his leave and the two men parted ways.

Roy trudged into his barracks and looked over at his desk. Instead of the usual clear workspace, a blue envelope was placed atop his desk, along with a small box. A letter had arrived—the letter he'd been waiting for!

Roy quickly sat down.

Dear Sir Roy,

It was her handwriting—how he'd missed her handwriting. He was ecstatic to see it again. Ah, so this was how desperately he'd been waiting for her letters. He felt the walls he'd built begin to crumble. A wave of longing washed over him. The small box next to the letter had already been opened, likely inspected for security. He felt regretful, as could tell it had been wrapped with care. His eyes widened as he opened the box to reveal a pen and an inkwell.

"Ah…" Her letter had mentioned a present. "I'll save this for special occasions only."

He vowed to hand his response to the messenger in person next time. Roy sat slowly rereading the letter, trying to calm his pounding heart. However, his heart continued to race late into the night.

Hiun beamed from ear to ear as he dismounted from his horse. The job was completed without a hitch and a sizable bonus awaited him, but there was something even better. He was finally returning with a response. He assumed it was another inspection when the soldiers at the security checkpoint had asked him to wait, but instead they handed him a letter. The stationery was coarse and thick, typical of what was used by soldiers. It was nothing compared to the finely scented stationery sent by the young lady, but that was of little importance. All that mattered was she was finally receiving a response.

Hiun passed the main house and headed straight towards Aris' quarters, located in the annex. He greeted the guards posted in front of Aris' room and knocked on the door.

"It's Hiun, my lady."

"Come in."

Entering the room, Hiun guessed Aris had bathed not long before, as she was seated while Lucine dried her hair.

Aris turned towards Hiun. "Was everything delivered safely?"

"Ah, the packaging of the box was opened because of the security inspection."

"That's too bad."

It would have been nice if it had arrived nicely wrapped.

"Also," Hiun said, the corners of his mouth breaking into a grin. "You've received a response."

At the word "response", Aris' eyes grew as wide as saucers. Hiun hastily pulled out the letter from his pocket and handed it to her.

"A response?" Aris said, her voice quivering as she held the letter. Roy had really written back to her. "I can't believe it."

She'd been sending the letters believing that she'd never get a reply, but he had written her a letter. She felt like she could cry. Just looking at the letter made her eyes well up with tears. It made her recall all the times she'd spent wracked with anxiety. How many times had she worried if he actually hated her letters?

"Ah," she breathed out shakily.

Lucine and Hiun smiled at Aris, before quickly leaving the room to give her some privacy. Once alone, she opened the envelope with trembling hands.

To Lady Aris Horissen,

His handwriting was steady and neat. She'd always known he was a real person, but he'd never felt more alive to her than in that moment while she held his letter in her hands. He wrote to her about life on the battlefield. He told her about Thurwin, a subordinate who never listened to him, and that he had received the bouquet she'd sent.

I smell the flowers every day and hope that the war will end soon. I don't particularly care for war.

He smells the flowers every day?

Aris suddenly felt bashful.

Your letters bring me peace and comfort.

They were just simple letters about her everyday life.

I am always eagerly awaiting your next letter.

Roy.

He ended the letter with this parting phrase. The precise handwriting reflected how much care he'd placed into writing the letter.

Aris sighed. She felt her eyes brimming with tears.

Reading the letter brought mixed feelings of happiness tinged with sadness. Now, they could both be able to write letters to each other. They would exchange letters and deepen their affection for each other. That was what they would do. Aris' heart fluttered at the mere thought.

"Roy," she whispered to herself as she started reading his letter again.

Her heart pounded.

Despite her best efforts to steady her heartbeat, it would not stop racing.

Continues In Volume 2

Printed in Great Britain
by Amazon